PRAISE for Monkey Town

"*Inherit the Wind* meets *To Kill a Mockingbird*, with a twist of E. L. Doctorow." —*San Francisco Chronicle*

★ "Weaving a somber yet witty narrative around a pivotal event, this fast-paced drama is reminiscent of Harper Lee's *To Kill a Mockingbird*. . . . An excellent read and a wonderful piece of literature." —*School Library Journal*, starred review

"A timely and engaging presentation of an early chapter in an ongoing national story." —*Horn Book*

★ "Readers . . . will be pleased by the depth of character and ideas here." —*Kirkus Reviews*, starred review

"The verdict is in. . . . The Scopes trial lives on in this mesmerizing novel." —James Carville

"Ronald Kidd brings alive the most famous trial of its time. . . ." —Richard Peck, author of *A Year Down Yonder*

"Captivating and thought-provoking." —*Chicago Sun-Times*

"With its lively dialogue, fast-paced plot, and adroit use of historical detail, *Monkey Town* is a welcome contribution and an important read." —*Geotimes*

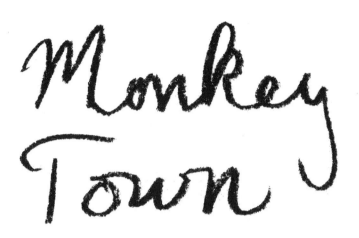

Monkey Town

THE SUMMER of the SCOPES TRIAL

Ronald Kidd

Simon Pulse
NEW YORK LONDON TORONTO SYDNEY

SIMON PULSE
An imprint of Simon & Schuster Children's Publishing Division
1230 Avenue of the Americas, New York, NY 10020
Text copyright © 2006 by Ronald J. Kidd
Illustrations of ape and pint glass copyright © csaimages.com
All rights reserved, including the right of reproduction in whole
or in part in any form.
All of the H. L. Mencken quotations copyright © 1925,
reprinted with the permission of the *Baltimore Sun*
SIMON PULSE and colophon are registered trademarks of Simon & Schuster, Inc.
Also available in a Simon & Schuster Books for Young Readers hardcover edition.
Designed by Jessica Sonkin
The text of this book was set in Galliard.
Manufactured in the United States of America
First Simon Pulse edition October 2007
10 9 8 7 6 5 4 3 2 1
The Library of Congress has cataloged the hardcover edition as follows:
Kidd, Ronald.
Monkey Town : the summer of the Scopes trial / by Ronald Kidd.—1st ed.
p. cm.
Summary: When her father hatches a plan to bring publicity to their small Tennessee town by arresting a local high school teacher for teaching about evolution, the resulting 1925 Scopes trial prompts fifteen-year-old Frances to rethink many of her beliefs about religion and truth, as well as her relationship with her father.
ISBN-13: 978-1-4169-0572-1 (hardcover, alk. paper)
ISBN-10: 1-4169-0572-3 (hardcover, alk. paper)
1. Scopes, John Thomas—Trials, litigation, etc.—Juvenile fiction. 2. Evolution—Study and teaching—Law and legislation—Tennessee—Juvenile fiction. [1.Scopes, John Thomas—Trials, litigation, etc.—Fiction. 2. Evolution—Study and teaching—Law and legislation—Fiction. 3. Fathers and daughters—Fiction. 4. Publicity—Fiction. 5. Tennessee—History—20th century—Fiction.] I. Title.
PZ7.K5315Mon 2006
[Fic]—dc22
2005008920
ISBN-13: 978-1-4424-4211-5

To Yvonne and Maggie,
who inspire me every day

To Craig Gabbert and his family,
who told me the story

And to Frances Robinson Gabbert,
who lived it

Prayer can accomplish a lot. It can cure diabetes, find lost pocket-books and restrain husbands from beating their wives. But is prayer made any more efficacious by giving a circus first? Coming to this thought, Dayton begins to sweat.

—H. L. Mencken
The Baltimore Evening Sun
July 9, 1925

PART 1
THE TOWN

PART 2
THE TRIAL

PART 3
THE TRUTH

PART ONE

THE TOWN

The town, I confess, greatly surprised me. . . . The houses are surrounded by pretty gardens, with cool green lawns and stately trees. The two chief streets are paved from curb to curb. The stores carry good stocks and have a metropolitan air, especially the drug, book, magazine, sporting goods and soda-water emporium of the estimable Robinson. A few of the town ancients still affect galluses and string ties, but the younger bucks are very nattily turned out. Scopes himself, even in his shirt sleeves, would fit into any college campus in America save that of Harvard alone.

—H. L. Mencken
The Baltimore Evening Sun
July 9, 1925

ONE

In my house the early bird didn't get the worm. It got the bathroom. There was one bathroom for four people, and if you weren't quick, you'd end up waiting outside the door. Today, of all days, I wasn't going to wait.

I climbed out of bed, grabbed my hairbrush, and hurried down the hall. Mama and Daddy's room was still dark. In the next room Sonny was all twisted up in his bedsheets, holding a teddy bear in one hand and a rubber tomahawk in the other.

So far so good.

I slipped into the bathroom and closed the door quietly. Setting my back against the door, I breathed a big sigh. Success!

I turned on the light and leaned over the sink to splash some water on my face. Staring up at me was a slimy green creature with bug eyes.

I screamed and ripped open the door. Sonny was standing there with his tomahawk.

"You scared him," said Sonny. He pushed past me and went to the sink.

I sputtered, "*I* scared *him?*"

Sonny lifted the creature out of the sink and cradled it in his hand. Meanwhile my parents came out of their bedroom, Daddy in his nightshirt and Mama pulling on a robe.

"Is everyone all right?" asked Daddy.

"No, we're not!" I said. "That thing scared the life out of me."

Sonny said, "It's not a thing. It's a chameleon."

I said, "This isn't a zoo. Tell him, Daddy."

"Now, sweetheart . . ."

Sonny went into the bathroom and shut the door.

"Hey, what are you doing?" I yelled.

A muffled voice said, "What do you think I'm doing?"

"Well, I'm next," I said.

Daddy said, "Frances, be a dear and let your mother go next. She needs to get breakfast started."

"But, Daddy—"

"Come to think of it," he said, "could I get in there and shave? I have to be at the store early this morning."

I said, "What about me? Johnny Scopes invited me to play tennis. I have to get ready."

"Call him *Mr.* Scopes," said Mama. "He's a teacher."

"Mama, I'm fifteen and he's twenty-four. We're practically the same age. Anyway, he said I could call him Johnny."

"In this house you'll call him Mr. Scopes," she said.

His full name was John Thomas Scopes, and I thought

he was the handsomest man I had ever seen. I had met him the summer before, in 1924, when he had first come to Dayton, Tennessee, where I lived. The school board had hired him as the football and basketball coach at Rhea Central High School, and Daddy, as chairman of the school board, had invited him to supper. Right there, over fried okra and corn bread, we had become friends. He had an easy way of talking, not just with Mama and Daddy but with me, too. He asked me questions and actually listened to the answers.

I found out that, besides being friendly, Johnny had traveled everywhere, including Illinois, Ohio, and Paducah, Kentucky. He had just graduated from college, and after working on a farm for a few weeks near his parents' home in Salem, Illinois, he had heard about the opening at our school.

That fall Johnny became one of the most popular teachers at Rhea Central. He had a yellow Dodge roadster, and on Saturday nights he would drive up to Morgan Springs, a resort community in the mountains above Dayton, where he would dance to the music of a live band. Some of the parents disapproved, especially the Baptists, but they came around when his football team almost beat our biggest rival, Baylor High School in Chattanooga.

Johnny was different from most people in Dayton. For him the world didn't begin and end on Market Street. It extended over the mountains, into strange and wonderful places, places I dreamed of going someday. Johnny felt the same way about ideas. He didn't like the small, familiar ones that people talked about in Dayton. He looked for ideas that would "stretch your mind," as he liked to say.

I wanted to stretch my mind, and I desperately wanted Johnny Scopes to help me.

The bathroom door opened, and Sonny came out, holding the chameleon. He asked me, "How are you going to play tennis with tin cans on your head?"

I said, "They're curlers. They make my hair look nice."

"I think it looks terrible."

"Frances," said Mama, "are you sure Mr. Scopes invited you?"

"Yes, I'm sure!"

"Well, I just don't want you pestering him."

Sonny grinned. "Frances loves Mr. Scopes, Frances loves Mr. Scopes."

I hit him on the arm. "Shut up, Sonny."

"Ow! Did you see what she did?"

Sonny stuck his tongue out at me. So did the chameleon. Daddy went to look for his razor. Mama disappeared into the bathroom. And me? I waited outside the door.

An hour later I headed downstairs to breakfast, wearing a tennis outfit and no curlers. On the way I stopped in the hall and checked the mirror. I pinched my cheeks to make them turn pink, which was the closest Mama let me come to using makeup. Then I stepped back and gazed at myself.

My face was round, with a high forehead that I tried to cover up with bangs. My hair was brown, almost black, and I wore it short the way lots of girls were starting to do. My eyes were brown too. I liked to think they were friendly eyes, the eyes of somebody you could trust. That was a big thing at our house. Daddy always said the world was divided into two kinds of people: the ones you could trust, and the ones you couldn't.

I tried out a smile. It came out more like a lopsided grin. I'd been working on it lately, hoping to make myself appear sophisticated and mysterious, but the truth was that I looked like somebody's kid sister, which is exactly how Johnny Scopes treated me. I was determined to change that, starting today.

When I got to the dining room, Daddy was sitting at our big round oak table reading the paper, with Sonny in his lap. Mama was just putting out a breakfast of scrambled eggs, sausage, biscuits, and gravy.

"I'll trade you a biscuit for that newspaper," she said.

"Yes, ma'am," said Daddy. He placed the newspaper on a round platform in the middle of the table and turned it until the paper reached Mama. About that same time the biscuits, also on the platform, came around to Daddy, and he popped one onto his plate. Daddy was always thinking of a better way to do things, and installing the platform, called a lazy Susan, on our dining table was one of his ideas.

I watched Daddy as he buttered his biscuit. In most ways he was a fairly ordinary-looking person. His hairline was receding. His ears were too big. His eyes were weak, so he wore wire-rimmed glasses that were constantly sliding down his nose. He wasn't a large man—in fact, you could almost call him short—but there was something about him that filled a room.

As Daddy took a bite of his biscuit, Mama dug into the newspaper. Unlike Daddy she really was large—not fat, mind you, just big. She had wide shoulders, big hips, and hair that was so long that when she took out her hairpins to brush it, the hair curled up in her lap like a sleepy black cat. I had tried to convince her to cut her hair short, the way most people did, but she wouldn't have any of it.

"I like what I like," she always said. That was just Mama's way.

In between cooking meals, making sandwiches for the store, and watching Sonny and me, Mama somehow found time for music. There was a piano in our parlor, where she would practice by herself or with friends for performances she put on all over town. She loved every kind of music from Bach to ragtime, and little by little she was teaching me how to play.

Daddy looked up from his biscuits. "Frances, can I count on you at the store today?"

"I told you, Daddy, I'm playing tennis. I need to be there at ten o'clock."

"Perfect," he said. "You can help out before you go."

"But school just got out. I haven't had a vacation yet."

He laughed. "Vacation? What's that?" He looked at Sonny. "What about you, young man? How would you like a turn at the soda fountain?"

"Yes, sir!"

I knew for a fact that Sonny would spend more time eating ice cream than serving it, but I didn't say anything.

After breakfast I helped Mama clear the dishes. Then Daddy, Sonny, and I headed off for another day at the store.

I didn't know it then, but that day would change things forever—for me, for Johnny Scopes, and for the town of Dayton, Tennessee. Nothing would ever again be as clear, as simple, as full of hope and promise as things seemed when I set out on that hot, lovely morning.

TWO

"Frances?" Daddy called. "Three Coca-Colas, please, ma'am."

"Yes, sir," I answered.

It was nine o'clock in the morning, and already Robinson's Drugs was busy. Old Mr. Clark wanted a remedy for his bunions. Mrs. Ott was looking for something to remove stains, while her four-year-old son, Floyd, raced around the store trying to make new ones. A group of businessmen huddled at the magazine rack, deciding what President Coolidge should do next.

Daddy weaved in and out among them, talking, laughing, listening to problems, offering advice. He ate and slept at home, but this was where he lived.

The door opened and in came Perry Swafford, a constable in the sheriff's office.

"Morning, Mr. Earle," he said. "Hot enough for you?" Daddy's name was Frank Earle Robinson, but everybody called him Mr. Earle.

Daddy grinned. "I'm not complaining. The hotter it

gets, the more Coca-Cola I sell. Speaking of which . . ."

He shot me a look. I hustled over to the soda fountain, stepping over Sonny, who was playing jacks behind the counter. I took three glasses from a nearby shelf, scooped ice into them, and pulled on a shiny metal handle. Out poured the bubbly brown liquid that Robinson's was known for.

Daddy always said Coca-Cola was the gasoline that made our engine run. It brought people into the store, and usually they would buy something else as long as they were there. He said Coca-Cola was the perfect drink. Besides tasting great, it was good for headaches, stomach problems, and general lethargy, which is the way you feel when you've had too much fried chicken.

I watched as the foam rose to the top of the first glass, being careful not to let it overflow. I nursed it higher and higher, waiting each time for the foam to subside, the way Daddy had taught me. Then I filled the other two glasses, set all three on a tray, and carried them to a table where Mr. Hicks was sitting.

"Thank you, Miss Frances," he said in a low voice, taking the glasses and arranging them in a circle in front of him. He smiled at them as if they were a group of old friends. Then he started to drink.

Mr. Hicks did the same thing every morning. He would stumble into the store, bleary-eyed, and make his way to the same table, where he ordered the same thing—three

Coca-Colas. He would line them up and drink them, and by the time he was done his eyes would be bright and he'd be swapping jokes with his friends, which included just about everybody in the store. Daddy said it was a testament to the medicinal powers of Coca-Cola.

Mr. Hicks was the city attorney, and his office was a few doors down the street. The interesting thing about Mr. Hicks was his name. It was Sue. That may sound funny, but personally I thought it was a pretty good name for a lawyer. Anyway, I liked Mr. Hicks because he could drink more Coca-Cola than anybody I ever saw. And I saw a lot of them.

People would come in for their Coca-Cola on the way to work, or halfway through the morning, or at lunchtime, or in the afternoon for a quick pick-me-up, or on the way home after work to cap off the day. Or, if you were Mr. Hicks, you'd come by at all those times, plus a few more for good measure. It always seemed to me that each time he came by he would talk a little faster, but that could have been my imagination.

George Rappleyea sat at the table next to him, reading the *Chattanooga Times*. Rappleyea was a nervous little man with wrinkled clothes and bad teeth, and he came from New York, which meant that he talked fast and had a strange accent. While traveling in Tennessee he had met a local girl, Miss Ova Corvin, and after marrying her had settled down in Dayton. It wasn't long before he got a job as manager of Cumberland Coal and Iron, a mining company that had fallen on hard times.

Rappleyea had a handful of people working for him, but mostly he managed company property and argued with folks. One of the few people who didn't mind was Daddy, who liked a good argument every now and then. He said it kept him on his toes.

Rappleyea called out, "Hey, Mr. Earle, I think I'll have a sandwich this morning. What have you got?"

"Same as always, George," said Daddy. "Tuna fish, chicken salad, pimento cheese, and the ham special."

"The ham special? What's in it?"

Daddy said, "Company secret. I can't reveal that information. The chef would kill me."

Rappleyea laughed. He and everybody else in town knew that the chef was my mother. "I'll take one," he said. "While you're at it, bring me a Coca-Cola."

Daddy motioned to me, and I scurried back to the soda fountain. Rappleyea, spotting something in the newspaper, showed it to a friend at the next table, and soon they were deep in conversation.

They weren't alone. Other than drinking Coca-Cola, talking was the main thing that went on at our store. People would sit at the wrought-iron tables and chairs, and they would catch up on the latest news of Dayton. They would discuss politics, town gossip, the strawberry crop, the coal mine—whatever was on their minds. Daddy always said that if something interesting happened in Dayton, within an hour people would be discussing it over a soda in our store.

Besides hearing about Dayton, you could find out what was going on in big cities like Chattanooga, Atlanta, Chicago, even New York, because Robinson's carried newspapers from around the country, stacked up by the window next to the sponges and shaving cream.

Daddy liked keeping up with events. He was a special correspondent for the *Chattanooga Times*, which meant he would call and tell the newspaper when anything good happened in Dayton. He was also chairman of the school board, a founding member of the Progressive Club, and the first person you'd go to if you needed a loan or a helping hand.

By nine forty-five that morning the store was filled with customers. Just as I was wondering when I'd ever be able to slip away, Billy Langford arrived. A nervous young man in his twenties with red hair and freckles, Billy was the store's one employee. He wasn't especially good with merchandise or people or even Coca-Colas, but he had one redeeming feature: He worshipped my father. Many times I would enter the store to find him literally sitting at my father's feet, soaking up Mr. Earle's views on every topic from advertising to philosophy.

I took off my apron and handed it to Billy. "It's a busy day," I said. "Good luck."

I told Daddy I was leaving, then grabbed my tennis racket and headed for the door. As I walked past George Rappleyea's table, I heard him say something about

Johnny Scopes. I glanced over and saw him gesturing excitedly.

Why would George Rappleyea be talking about Johnny Scopes? They barely knew each other.

Edging closer, I tried to hear more but couldn't make it out. Then I looked up at the clock. It was almost ten. I cast one more glance at Rappleyea and moved toward the door.

I hurried down Main Street, stopping every few steps to practice my tennis strokes. When I turned left on Cedar, I could see the outlines of the high school in the distance. There was an old clay tennis court in back where Johnny had said we could play.

Coming around the side of the school, I made out Johnny at one end of the court, practicing his serve. I stopped for a moment to admire him. He was tall and thin, with rounded-off shoulders and an easy way of moving. When he hit the ball, his blond hair flopped down over his forehead, and he pushed it back with his free hand.

As I watched him, my mind wandered. It was three years in the future, and I was just graduating high school. I came off the stage wearing a cap and gown, and waiting at the bottom of the steps was Johnny Scopes. Smiling, he scooped me into his arms and carried me to his yellow Dodge roadster. Then we drove off toward the hills to begin our new life together. We would live in a city, meet lots of people, and explore the wide world. I would leave my old life behind—the small town, the small minds, the small thoughts.

The best part was that I wouldn't be Frances Robinson anymore. I would be Mrs. Johnny Scopes.

Coming back to the present, I flashed my best smile and called out, "Hi, Johnny. I made it."

He grinned and waved back. "Hello, Frances. We were just getting started."

We?

Johnny hit another serve, and I looked out from around the building to see who was on the other side of the net. When I did, my stomach tightened and my fists clenched. It was Myrna Maxwell.

Myrna watched the ball skip past her. "Ooh, Johnny, you are so good!" she said.

She minced off after the ball, using delicate little steps that were more suited to a dance floor than a tennis court. Myrna had graduated a couple of years before and had stayed around town, looking for eligible men. Johnny was her latest project.

Johnny trotted over to me, and Myrna joined him presently. "Hi, kiddo," he said. "Do you know Myrna Maxwell?"

"Coca-Cola float, one scoop of ice cream."

Myrna laughed. "I don't have many floats these days. I'm trying to watch my waistline."

"Really?" I said. "You order one practically every day."

Johnny said, "If it wasn't for Myrna I'd be home in Illinois by now. She invited me to a potluck at her church this Sunday, so I decided to stay around town for a little while longer."

I tried to smile. I had hoped the reason Johnny stayed was me. The thought that it was Myrna dug into my skin like a burr.

"Do you play tennis?" asked Myrna.

"Yes, I do," I said, gritting my teeth.

She said, "You could play with us if you want—you know, girls against the boys." Myrna winked at Johnny, and he grinned.

Yes, Myrna, I thought. *I could play with you and Johnny. I could also wring your neck.*

"You go ahead and play," I told her. "Maybe we could take turns."

Johnny said, "As long as you brought your racket, could Myrna use it? She's having trouble with hers."

Biting my tongue, I handed Myrna the racket. She smiled. "That is so sweet."

And that's how I ended up watching Myrna Maxwell use my racket to play tennis with Johnny Scopes. Of course, the game Myrna was playing with Johnny wasn't really tennis. She kept missing the ball on purpose and asking Johnny for help. When he came around to her side of the net, she got him to stand behind her, put his hand on hers, and demonstrate the swing. It made me sick.

Johnny didn't want someone who was helpless. He wanted a real tennis partner, one who would stand her ground, return his shots, maybe even hit one by him every now and then. Watching Myrna, it was all I could do to keep from charging onto the court and grabbing the racket.

Mercifully, the demonstration didn't last long. A few minutes later my brother came running up, shouting, "Mr. Scopes! Mr. Scopes!"

Johnny lowered his racket. "What is it, Sonny?"

"My father needs to see you at the store right away," Sonny replied. "It's about your job."

THREE

Johnny apologized to Myrna, saying he would call her later, and raced off to Robinson's Drugs, with Sonny leading the way. I retrieved my tennis racket and joined them.

As we headed across town, Sonny called out, "Make way! Coming through!" He was on an important mission and wanted to make sure everyone knew it.

I heard a girl's voice. "Frances? Frances, wait!"

It was Eloise Purser, my best friend, who lived across the street from us on Market. A thin, dark-haired girl, Eloise had a sly smile and was always ready for fun.

Catching up with us, she said, "Can I come with you?"

"You don't even know where we're going," I said.

She grinned. "No, but I'd like to find out."

We flew down Market Street, past the Rhea County Courthouse, a redbrick building with a clock tower on top and lawns stretching out on all sides. It was the official county seat, but a lot of people thought the true center of Dayton was Robinson's Drugs.

When we entered the store a few minutes later, we saw Daddy sitting with some men at one of the tables. Looking up, Daddy motioned and said, "Johnny, come on over here."

Johnny approached them, while Eloise and I took seats at the soda fountain. Sonny tried to tag along with Johnny until I grabbed the back of his britches and hoisted him up onto my lap.

"Hey, why'd you do that?" he squawked.

"Shh!" I said. "This may be important."

Sitting beside Daddy was George Rappleyea, his newspaper folded up on the table. Next to him was Sue Hicks, sucking on a Coca-Cola as usual. Rounding out the group was Walter White, superintendent of the Rhea County schools. Seeing the school superintendent, I remembered what Sonny had told Johnny at the tennis court: *It's about your job.*

"Have a seat, boy," said Daddy, offering Johnny his chair. Johnny, faced with the two men who had hired him, did as he was told.

Daddy turned to Billy Langford. "Billy, bring him a Coca-Cola, please."

"Yes, sir, Mr. Earle!" said Billy. He brought the drink, and Daddy got down to business.

"Johnny," he said, "we thought you could clear up a question for us. We were just wondering whether a person could teach high school biology without talking about evolution."

"Well, sir," said Johnny, "it's possible but not likely. I'll show you what I mean."

Now, it just so happened that Daddy, besides being chairman of the school board, was also the local textbook distributor. Johnny walked over to one of the shelves and picked out a book called *Civic Biology*, by George W. Hunter, which he thumbed through until he found what he was looking for.

"See, here's a whole section on evolution and Charles Darwin," he said, showing them the pages. "This is the state-approved textbook, so it would be pretty hard to teach biology without mentioning it."

That seemed to get everybody all excited. As they looked through the book, Sonny pulled on my sleeve and said, "What are they talking about?"

"If you'll be quiet for a minute, maybe we'll find out," I told him.

Walter White took off his glasses. "So, Johnny, you're telling us you taught evolution?"

"Every teacher in the state taught evolution if they used this book."

"Yes," said Sue Hicks, leaning forward, "but did you?"

"Sue, I'm the football and basketball coach, and I teach a little physics and math. The only time I taught biology was in the spring, when Mr. Ferguson was sick for a few days. I used this book, so I suppose I may have covered evolution."

George Rappleyea sat back in his chair and grinned. "Mr.

Earle, I think we've got our man. Where's the constable?"

"Constable?" said Johnny.

"That's right," Rappleyea said. "We're going to arrest you."

Johnny half-rose from his seat, knocking his Coca-Cola into Walter White's lap. White stood up, sputtering. Eloise and I glanced at each other, trying hard not to laugh. Walter White worked hard at looking dignified, and now he would have to walk around town with wet pants.

Billy Langford, who had been watching, rushed over and began patting White's lap with a napkin.

"Get away from me!" said White.

"Thank you, Billy, that's fine," Daddy said. Reaching into the pocket of his pharmacist's coat, he pulled out a slip of paper and handed it to White. "Walter, here's a free coupon for the dry cleaner. I like to keep 'em handy for spills."

Daddy turned back to the others and said, "Gentlemen, maybe we should tell Mr. Scopes what's going on here."

"I'd certainly appreciate it," Johnny said, sitting back down.

"You've heard of the Butler Act?" asked Sue Hicks. Fueled by energy from a dozen Coca-Colas, he went on without waiting for an answer. "It was passed a couple of months ago. Makes it illegal in the state of Tennessee to teach evolution, or any other theory that denies the creation of man as taught in the Bible."

"That's why you're going to arrest me?" asked Johnny.

Daddy said, "Son, no one's going to arrest you if you don't agree to it. We just had an idea and thought you might be interested. Or, rather, George had an idea. Show him, George."

He turned to Rappleyea, who pulled out his copy of the *Chattanooga Times* and pointed to an article on a back page.

PLAN ASSAULT
ON STATE LAW
ON EVOLUTION

CIVIL LIBERTIES UNION
TO FILE TEST CASE

Rappleyea ran his finger down the article and read, "'A legal test of the Tennessee law prohibiting the teaching of evolution in public schools and colleges is being sought by the American Civil Liberties Union, a national free speech organization, according to Professor Clarence R. Skinner, of Tufts College, chairman of the union's committee on academic freedom. "We are looking for a Tennessee teacher who is willing to accept our services in testing this law in the courts," Professor Skinner states. "Our lawyers think a friendly test case can be arranged without costing a teacher his or her job. . . . All we need now is a willing client."'"

Rappleyea looked up at Johnny and grinned. "That's you, bub," he said.

"His name isn't bub," Sonny piped up, and I poked him with my finger.

"Why don't you get Mr. Ferguson?" asked Johnny. "He taught biology all year long."

"He's the school principal," said Walter White, "and he has a wife and children."

Johnny said, "Why do we have to do this at all? Let Chattanooga or Nashville handle it."

"Oh, they will if we let them," said Rappleyea. "And we'll miss the best chance we ever had."

"Look, Johnny," said Daddy, "you're new to Dayton, so I wouldn't expect you to understand. You know how many people lived here in 1890? Three thousand. You know how many live here now?"

"I'm not sure," said Johnny.

"About half that many. People lit out of here by the hundreds when Cumberland Coal and Iron shut down their blast furnace. We've still got farming and a couple of small factories, but other than that we're hurting, son. Now, we've got a beautiful little town here, but nobody outside Rhea County knows it. The way I see it, there's just one solution."

He looked at Johnny, waiting for an answer, as if he were the teacher and Johnny were the student. Johnny shrugged. "More people?"

"Right. And how do you get more people? More business. And how do you get more business? Publicity, boy, publicity."

Nearby, Billy Langford beamed. In his conversations with my father, publicity was one of his favorite topics. Many times I had seen Daddy offer a free Coca-Cola to the local newspaper editor, Seth Folsom, and then bend his ear about the store's latest sale or product line.

George Rappleyea explained to Johnny, "If we hold the test case here, people all over the country will read about Dayton, including business owners. If they like what they read, maybe some of them will decide to move their businesses here."

"You can put Dayton on the map," said Daddy, "and all you have to do is say yes. We'll take care of everything else."

Daddy was good at taking care of things. In a way it was what he did best. But there was something different about the way he was saying it now, something that made me wonder. Would it really be that easy for Johnny? Could he just say yes and forget about it? If it was so important, could Daddy handle it with just a snap of his fingers?

Johnny looked around the table, trying to decide. As he did, something amazing happened. Robinson's Drugs, where no one ever stopped talking, suddenly became quiet. It was as if the place were holding its breath, waiting for an answer. Johnny studied the faces around the table, searching for clues or maybe for help. The screen door creaked. The air hummed. The ceiling fans turned, mixing the smells of bacon and soap and tobacco.

All of a sudden I had the feeling something momentous

was happening. The wind had changed, the ground was shifting, and in the middle of it all sat Johnny Scopes. For a moment everything was silent. Then the moment passed.

"Do you have to arrest me?" Johnny asked. "I've never been to jail in my life."

Sue Hicks chuckled. "There won't be any jail. The arrest is just a formality. You'll be free to go wherever you want."

"What about my job?" asked Johnny.

"Son, your job is to beat Baylor High in football next year," said Daddy, "and we'll make sure you're still around to do that. Right, Walter?"

"Huh? Oh, right," mumbled Walter White, who seemed more interested in wiping off his pants.

"So, what do you say?" asked Daddy. "You'd be doing a service to every man, woman, and child in Dayton."

"Well," Johnny said, "when you put it that way, how can I say no?"

Daddy slapped him on the back. "Attaboy! I knew we could count on you."

And that's how it all started.

FOUR

After the meeting, Daddy got on the telephone and called some newspapers in Chattanooga and Nashville. George Rappleyea sent a telegram to the American Civil Liberties Union. Meanwhile, word spread quickly around Dayton. By the time Daddy, Sonny, and I got home that night Mama knew all about it. She gave Daddy an earful at supper.

"You actually had him arrested?" she asked.

"Aw, sugar, it doesn't mean a thing," said Daddy between bites of fried chicken.

"It's a formality," I explained.

"Oh, I see," said Mama.

Sonny said, "He was teaching revolution."

"Evolution," I corrected him. "It's a theory that says people came from monkeys."

Sonny laughed. "I came from monkeys." He scratched under his arms and made whooping sounds.

"Sonny!" said Mama.

Daddy tried to keep from smiling. "That's enough, young man."

Mama said, "The theory was by an Englishman named Charles Darwin. He said people weren't present when the world began. There was no Adam and Eve or Garden of Eden—just some little one-celled animals. From those animals came bigger animals, and after millions of years came man."

"What about the monkeys?" asked Sonny.

"Evolutionists say that people are closely related to monkeys. They say we're just another kind of animal."

"Is it true?" asked Sonny.

Daddy said, "Read your Bible. How long did it take God to make the world?"

"I don't know," said Sonny. "A year?"

"Seven days," Daddy said.

"Six," said Mama. "Then he rested."

Daddy winked at me. "He didn't own a drug store."

Mama said, "God made man in his own image. Monkeys had nothing to do with it."

"If evolution isn't true, why did they put it in the textbook?" I asked.

"Some people believe it," said Mama.

"Who?"

"Nobody around here. Well, maybe old Mr. Davis, the printer. He likes to be different."

"The point is," said Daddy, "it's against the law to

teach it, at least in Tennessee. We're going to use that to put Dayton on the map."

That got Mama going again. "By arresting an innocent young man, then bringing in outsiders to run the trial?" she asked. "What kind of crazy idea is that?"

"It's not crazy; it's a stroke of genius," said Daddy. "During the trial people all over the country are going to read about how nice Dayton is. Mark my words, it'll bring new business to town."

Mama said, "If you ask me, it's a bunch of foolishness."

"This is going to be the biggest thing that ever hit Dayton," said Daddy. "Just you wait and see."

That was Tuesday. By Wednesday things had started to happen. The American Civil Liberties Union sent a telegram back to George Rappleyea saying they would pay for Johnny's defense. On Thursday the *Nashville Banner* ran a front-page article about the trial, and by Friday the story had been picked up by newspapers across the country. Everybody was reading about Dayton, just the way Daddy had said.

On Saturday there was a preliminary hearing at the courthouse, where Arthur Benson and the other justices of the peace officially decided what everybody already knew—that the trial would go on. The next step, when Johnny was supposed to appear before a grand jury, wouldn't take place until August, so Johnny decided he would leave on Monday morning to spend the summer back home in Illinois.

I hated the thought of spending the summer without him. I'd gotten used to seeing him just about every day at school. I would think of an excuse to drop by the gym or the practice field, and we'd talk while he finished up for the day. Then he would gather up his things and walk me home. He lived at Bailey's boardinghouse, a rambling place down the street from our house, conveniently located just a block from school.

When we got to my house, he would do the same thing every day. He would say, "Good night, Frances," and ruffle my hair with his hand. It was the kind of thing you'd do with your little sister, and I was determined to change it.

I tried a more sophisticated hairstyle. I practiced my most alluring smile in front of the mirror. I even dabbed on a little makeup. I pictured him, silhouetted against the late afternoon sky, leaning down and kissing me gently. I longed for that moment with all my heart, but so far it hadn't happened. Monday would be my last chance of the summer.

On Sunday I baked some chocolate chip cookies and put them in a box under my bed. When Monday morning arrived, I got out my nicest dress and tied a ribbon in my hair, then took the box from under my bed and headed for Bailey's boardinghouse.

I found Johnny in front, packing up his yellow Dodge roadster. There were suitcases and boxes jammed into every part of the car.

"Hi, kiddo," he said. "What are you doing here?"

I hated the word "kiddo" almost as much as getting my hair ruffled, but I tried not to show it.

"I just came to say good-bye," I said. "I won't be seeing you for the rest of summer."

Johnny chuckled. "I think you'll survive." He loaded more boxes into the car and hung a baseball glove on the gearshift knob.

"What are you going to do with that glove?" I asked him.

"You never know when you'll come across a ball game," he said. "I stopped for one on my way here last summer, and they invited me to supper. Took me three days to get to Dayton."

"Speaking of supper, how was the potluck at Myrna's church?" I asked. I'd been waiting for an opening to ask him about it.

He said, "I've never seen so many casseroles in my life. Myrna baked a chess pie."

"Was it good?" I asked.

"Delicious."

"I hate chess pie."

Johnny smiled. "She tried to talk me into staying here for the summer. I told her I couldn't. She seemed a little upset."

"Poor thing," I said.

I pulled out the box and handed it to him. "Here's a little going-away present."

"Really? For me?"

He took the box, and his smile softened. He gazed down at me with a thoughtful look on his face. I could see us in ten years, sitting on a porch, holding hands, sipping lemonade and making plans. Could he see it too?

I said, "I'll be thinking of you, Johnny. Whenever you open this box, maybe you'll remember me."

He took the top off the box. A fat green frog hopped out.

Johnny burst out laughing. I looked in the box. The cookies were gone.

I heard a familiar giggle from behind a tree, and I whirled around. "Sonny Robinson, I'm going to kill you!"

I turned back to Johnny. "There were chocolate chip cookies, I swear."

Sonny came out from behind the tree, his mouth smeared with chocolate. "Where's my frog? Roscoe? Roscoe, here, boy."

I took a step toward Roscoe, and Sonny held me back with his arm. "Don't move. You might squish him."

I said, "I'll squish you, you little worm."

Johnny grinned. "Thanks for the present, kids."

I said, "It was from me, not from us. And it was cookies."

A green shape hopped across the yard. Sonny said, "There he is!" He grabbed the box from Johnny and took off after the frog. I sighed.

Johnny said, "It was swell of you to come see me off."

"It should be an interesting summer," I said. "You're famous. People all around the country know your name."

"You think so?" he asked.

"They're calling it the Monkey Trial. You should see the newspapers—Chicago, St. Louis, Baltimore. Daddy's got them down at the store."

"It's starting to worry me," Johnny said.

"Why?"

"Did you go to the county fair last year?" he asked.

"Mama and Daddy took us on the train."

"You remember the Fun Zone? They had something called a roller coaster."

"I surely do," I said. "Daddy and I rode on it."

"So did I. I didn't like it."

"I thought you enjoyed going fast," I said.

He nodded toward his car. "I do if I'm driving. The frightening thing about a roller coaster is that someone else is in control. You go whipping around—up and down, around corners, and there's nothing you can do to change it. You just have to hang on until the ride is over." He shook his head, then looked down at me. "Frances, I have a funny feeling I just stepped onto a roller coaster."

"You'll be okay," I said. "Daddy won't let anything bad happen."

He still seemed worried, so I tried to cheer him up. "Well," I said, "at least this is one ride you won't have to pay for."

He gazed off down the street, where the courthouse tower rose above the trees. "I'm not so sure about that," he said.

FIVE

The minute Johnny left town, things started to go wrong.

It seemed that some folks in Chattanooga were jealous of the publicity that little Dayton was getting, so they decided to hold a trial of their own. They arrested a man for teaching evolution and scheduled the trial to take place before ours.

"By God, they've hijacked our trial!" said Daddy when he saw the paper that morning.

"And good riddance," Mama said.

"What's going to happen?" I asked Daddy.

"You know all those reporters who've been sniffing around town the past few days?" he said. "They'll pull up stakes and go to Chattanooga, unless we do something about it."

"Like what?" I said.

"Just watch."

Daddy called an emergency meeting of the Dayton Progressive Club, a group of business people who got together once a month for lunch at the Aqua Hotel, mostly to swap stories. This time they actually had something to talk about. They decided to hold a public protest meeting the next day so folks in Dayton could tell how they felt about the city of Chattanooga stealing their trial. At the protest meeting the Progressives would announce a boycott of Chattanooga goods, which meant we wouldn't buy anything made in that city, as a way of showing how we felt.

As usual, Mama had her doubts.

"What makes you think anybody's going to notice?" she asked Daddy at supper that night. "The reporters have left town. We'll just be talking to ourselves."

"Oh, they'll come back," he said, buttering his corn bread. "We've put out word that George Rappleyea's giving a speech in favor of evolution, which ought to stir up the crowd. And we might just have something else up our sleeves. You never know."

He smiled mysteriously. Mama just shook her head.

After supper I helped Mama clear the dishes, then went into the parlor and sat down at the piano. It was big and long and made of oak, with vines carved on the sides. Daddy had bought it for Mama when they got married, and it had been sitting in the parlor ever since.

If the store was Daddy's headquarters, the parlor was Mama's. It was the kind of room where you could lean back and relax—a little cluttered but cozy, with a comfortable sofa, a large window in front, and lots of wood paneling. Mama always kept two or three vases filled with cut flowers from the garden, so the room smelled of furniture polish and roses. The scent followed her around wherever she went, like a perfume.

Besides the piano, Mama had set up a big desk at the front window so she could read or work while watching us in the yard. Sonny and I would be outside playing stickball or marbles, and we'd look up to see Mama gazing at us through that window, like the captain of a ship.

I practiced my scales, then started in on the latest piece Mama was teaching me, Beethoven's *Moonlight Sonata*. I loved the way it sounded when she played it, all solemn and shimmery, but when I tried it, the notes kept getting in the way.

"Sit up straight, dear," she called from the kitchen. "Arch your wrists."

"You can't even see me," I called back, but of course she was right. How she did that I'll never know.

Sitting up straight, I arched my wrists and tried again. It didn't sound like Mama, but this time maybe there was a glimmer of moonlight.

The next morning the Progressive Club set up a speaker's stand in front of the courthouse, and by noon a good-size crowd had gathered on the lawn, including some of the same reporters who had left town the day before. Eloise Purser and I found a spot near the front.

"I heard somebody's going to talk about evolution," she said. "Some New Yorker. At least that's what they say."

"He lives here," I said. "It's George Rappleyea. He manages Cumberland Coal and Iron."

"You think he really believes we came from monkeys?"

"I guess so. Else he wouldn't be talking about it."

Eloise sniffed. "My father says it's an abomination."

"Then why is it in the textbook?" I said.

"Huh?"

"You were at the store that day. Remember what Johnny said? There's a section on evolution in our science textbook. If it's wrong, why did they put it there?"

"Frances, what are you talking about?"

"It's the book our teachers use. Johnny used it."

"Yes," said Eloise, "and they arrested him for it."

"That was just for publicity," I said.

"He was supposed to teach that God made the world in seven days, like it says in the Bible. He broke the law."

I said, "Maybe the law is wrong."

Eloise stared at me. "If the law is wrong, then so is the Bible. So are my parents and your parents and everybody else in town. Is that what you're saying, Frances? Do you really believe that?"

Suddenly I felt as if everyone were watching me, not just Eloise but the whole town of Dayton. I don't know why, but it made me mad. "Do you really think we're perfect?" I asked. "You think nobody in Dayton makes mistakes? Well, I live here too, and I see plenty of mistakes. People drive too fast on Main Street. Mr. Beasley has a bad wig. Mrs. Cowell dresses her poodle in skirts, and it's disgusting. Maybe the law *is* wrong. Maybe we're all wrong, and we just don't know it."

Eloise gave me a funny look. But before she could answer, a shout went up from the crowd, and Sue Hicks climbed onto the platform to start the festivities. I could tell Sue had already had a few Coca-Colas, because he was talking fast and pounding his fist into his palm. The subject was Chattanooga. He accused them of dirty tactics, and by the time he finished, the people were yelling and carrying on like they were at a football game.

Next, Gordon McKenzie announced the boycott of anything made in Chattanooga, and the crowd cheered its approval. Of course, by that time they were so whipped up that if he'd asked them to, they would have marched to Chattanooga and attacked the city with butter knives.

Finally George Rappleyea rose to speak. Next to me I saw Eloise perk up.

As usual, Rappleyea looked a little strange. His hair was piled up on top of his head like a stack of pancakes, and he kept fooling with his glasses.

"First of all," he began, "let me just say that I believe in the theory of evolution."

A group in back started to boo. When I turned around to look, I was amazed to see it was Daddy and his friends from the Progressive Club.

As Rappleyea continued, the Progressive Club kept up its racket. Soon the people around them joined in. Somebody yelled out, "What about the Bible?"

"It's not about the Bible," said Rappleyea. "It's a question of science. Our children deserve to hear the truth, and that's what John Scopes was teaching them."

Rappleyea went on to say that the Butler Act was wrong and that this trial would prove it once and for all. The more he talked, the louder the crowd got, until he was having to shout to be heard. The strange thing was that he almost seemed to be enjoying it. Instead of ignoring the crowd, he listened to their taunts and answered, saying things that were sure to make people mad. He even said that his ancestors were monkeys, and he didn't care who knew it.

". . . and speaking of monkeys," he added, "there are more monkeys here in Dayton than there are in the Chattanooga Zoo."

There was a commotion behind us, and a man yelled, "You can't call my ancestors monkeys!"

I turned and saw that it was Thurlow Reed, one of the barbers whose shop was across from Daddy's store. He pushed his way through the crowd and took a swing at George Rappleyea. Rappleyea ducked and threw a headlock on him. Thurlow struggled and, unable to get loose, bit Rappleyea on the arm.

I edged forward to see what happened next, but all of a

sudden somebody grabbed hold of Eloise and me and yanked us backward.

It was Mama. She dragged us over the lawn, out of the crowd, and across the street to our house, where she and Sonny had been watching from the front porch. Sonny, seeing us approach, jumped up and down, clapping his hands.

"A fight, a fight!" he said. "Who's winning?"

"Never you mind," said Mama. "It's foolishness. That's all you need to know."

At first I was a little upset at her because I'd been hoping to see what the crowd would do. As it turned out, though, we didn't miss much. We watched from the porch as Perry Swafford from the sheriff's office broke things up and sent people home.

It wasn't until later that I started wondering about the fight. After all, I had always thought Thurlow Reed and George Rappleyea were friends. I asked Daddy about it at the store that afternoon. He just smiled.

Next to him, Billy Langford grinned. "The power of publicity," he crowed.

"Now, you hush," said Daddy, but I could tell he wasn't really upset.

The next day Dayton was back in the news, just as Daddy had predicted. Newspapers around the country carried the story of Thurlow Reed, "the man-biting barber." Thurlow didn't seem to mind. In fact, he cut out the stories and put them on the wall of his barber shop.

That very same day there was another story in the paper. It said the Chattanooga teacher had denied talking about evolution, and the charges against him had been dropped. It seemed there wasn't going to be a Chattanooga trial after all.

Eloise and I read about it at the store, seated back-to-back on the floor next to a stack of newspapers.

"Nothing about this trial is real," I said. "It wasn't a real fight, and Johnny Scopes isn't a real biology teacher."

"Does it matter?" asked Eloise.

I said, "It's a lie, isn't it?"

"I think it's exciting," she said. "Look at these papers—New York, Boston, Atlanta. They're all writing about Dayton. It's publicity. Isn't that what you said?"

I didn't answer. I was thinking about my father, who believed in the power of publicity and always said it was wrong to tell a lie.

SIX

We sold a lot of Coca-Colas that day. It seemed that everybody in town stopped by to shake Daddy's hand and talk about the man-biting barber. Thurlow Reed himself spent a good part of the day at the front table, telling the story of his scuffle with George Rappleyea. Every time he told it the story got better, until in the last version he chased Rappleyea up a tree, which made Thurlow wonder if Rappleyea's ancestors really had been monkeys.

Sonny and I were working the soda fountain that afternoon, or rather I was working and Sonny was fooling around. While I served up Coca-Colas, he had gotten the bright idea of mixing a special drink. He had pulled out a glass and was going down the row of brightly colored syrups, pouring a little bit of each into the glass and stirring them with a long spoon to make an evil-looking green concoction. He was just adding soda water when Sue Hicks came bursting through the front door, waving a piece of paper, his face flushed with excitement.

"Mr. Earle," he yelled, "look at this!"

Heads turned, and people stopped talking. They watched as Daddy came out from behind the counter and took the paper, which I now could see was a telegram. Tipping his glasses down on his nose, Daddy read, "'To the honorable Sue K. Hicks, City Attorney, Dayton, Tennessee. From the editor, *Memphis Press.*'"

He looked up at Sue and said, "What's this? More publicity?"

"Keep reading," said Sue, glancing around the store. "Make sure everybody can hear it."

Daddy continued in a louder voice. "The telegram says 'Will you be willing for William Jennings Bryan to aid the state in the prosecution of J. T. Scopes?'"

There was a collective gasp, and then a cheer. People yelled and stomped and waved their hats. Sue responded with a deep bow.

It took a lot to catch my father off guard, but Sue had succeeded. Daddy stared at him. "William Jennings Bryan?"

Sue grinned and shouted over the crowd, "The Memphis folks say he's willing if we are. It's going to be big, Mr. Earle, it's going to be big."

As the noise died down, Sonny pulled on Daddy's sleeve. "Who's William Jennings Bryan?" he asked.

Daddy crouched down next to Sonny and said, "He may be the most famous man in America. He was secretary of state and was almost elected president. Now he travels around the country making speeches. They call him the Great Commoner."

Sue added, "He spoke in Memphis just the other day. Said evolution was wrong and the Bible was right. And now he's coming to Dayton! Talk about your publicity! Whooee! This calls for a Coca-Cola."

Sonny handed him a glass. Sue took a gulp, and his eyes got big. "This isn't Coca-Cola," he said.

Sue was right. In the excitement, Sonny had given him the wrong glass. The one Sue was holding contained Sonny's special drink.

Sue stood there, one hand on the glass and the other on his stomach. His forehead was all bunched up, and his eyebrows danced. The expression on his face reminded me of the time Daddy bit into an apple and found half a worm.

Sue turned to Sonny and gazed at him for a few moments. Then he let out a belch that rocked the shelves.

"I like it," he said.

I don't know where the idea came from, but all of a sudden I knew what Sonny's drink should be called.

I said, "It's a Monkey Fizz."

Daddy threw back his head and laughed. Sue joined in, and so did I. Sonny laughed too, but mostly he looked relieved.

"A Monkey Fizz," said Daddy. "That's good. That's very good."

"Maybe we could serve one to William Jennings Bryan when he comes to town," I said.

Daddy chuckled, then grew thoughtful. "You know, Frances, you might have something there. The reporters would love it." He turned to my brother. "Sonny, would you show me how to make one of those?"

"Yes, sir!" said Sonny.

As Sue headed off to discuss the telegram, Sonny led Daddy and me to the soda fountain. "Pay attention now," Sonny told us. "This is very scientific."

I said, "It was an accident. You don't even remember how to do it."

Ignoring me, he took a glass from the shelf and began pouring colored syrups into it. "The red syrup is for energy. Green is to make you smart. Blue helps you see better."

"See better?" I said.

"But the yellow syrup is the most important," said Sonny, looking at me. "It makes you be kind to children and small animals."

He stirred up the drink and added soda water, making it brown and bubbly, then put in a straw and handed it to me.

I wrinkled up my nose. "You really want me to drink this?"

Daddy said, "We can't serve it if we don't try it ourselves." He took a sip from the straw and leaned back thoughtfully. "Mmm. Kind of a cross between . . . ginger ale and blueberry pie."

Hesitantly I put in another straw and took a sip. Daddy and Sonny watched me for a reaction.

Suddenly I pointed out the window. "Look! Across the street, on that telephone pole—two gnats are kissing."

"Wow!" said Sonny. "It really does make you see better!"

He raced around the store, telling everybody about it. Daddy fixed up a sign and put it in the window. And who do you think got the privilege of standing behind the counter and mixing up batches of Monkey Fizz?

That's right. Yours truly.

Whenever there was big news, people would gather outside Robinson's before it opened, waiting to buy newspapers. They were there the next day, and they weren't disappointed. All the papers, including the *Memphis Press*, had articles about William Jennings Bryan coming to Dayton. People lined up halfway around the block to buy a paper and read about it.

As I sat at the soda fountain reading the articles, it dawned on me that what was good news for Dayton might be bad news for Johnny Scopes. With William Jennings Bryan against him, did he really have a chance?

As it turned out, I shouldn't have worried. Later that day a telegram came from Clarence Darrow, who, Daddy explained, was the most famous lawyer in the country. Darrow had read about Bryan and was offering to represent Johnny at the trial, free of charge.

Daddy cackled with glee when he heard about it. "It's a match made in heaven. Bryan believes in the Bible, and Darrow doesn't believe in anything."

"How can he not believe in anything?" I asked.

"That's what he claims," said Daddy. "Says he doesn't know if there's a God. But he's one heck of a lawyer. He'll give Bryan a run for his money. The press will eat it up."

"But what if Darrow wins?" asked Billy Langford.

"Oh, he's not going to win," said Daddy. "Don't you worry about that."

Daddy couldn't wait for things to get started. I guess the judge agreed. His name was John Raulston, and he was born in a town called Fiery Gizzard, Tennessee. Instead of waiting until August, the way he had originally planned, Judge Raulston showed up in town a few days later and announced that the grand jury would be held right away. The grand jury wasn't the trial itself but a quick hearing to see if the charges were strong enough to justify a trial.

Judge Raulston called together the local lawyers on both sides, along with a jury he quickly had rounded up, and they heard three students testify that Johnny Scopes really had taught evolution. That was enough for the jury, who decided the trial should go on.

People in town had figured we would have the whole summer to get ready for the big event, but the judge changed all that. When the grand jury was over, he declared that the trial would begin on July tenth, just six weeks away.

SEVEN

On a hilltop south of town was a creaky old house that everybody called the Mansion. Built by Cumberland Coal and Iron, it originally had been used by out-of-town executives when they came to Dayton. Since then, both the company and the Mansion had fallen on hard times.

The Mansion, deserted now, had eighteen rooms and was painted a weathered brown with yellow trim. The plumbing didn't work, and neither did the electricity. Even so, people said that on moonless nights you could sometimes see lights moving around the house. Because of that, kids from town liked to go up there on Halloween. More than one claimed to have seen ghosts.

Early in June, a few weeks after the trial date had been set, Billy Langford was off from work one day, so Daddy asked me to deliver a prescription to old Mrs. Cate, who lived just down the hill from the Mansion. I rode my bicycle to her house and dropped off the medicine. As I was leaving, I glanced up at the Mansion and thought I saw something move. If it had been nighttime I surely would have raced back to town, but the sky was bright and I was feeling brave, so I climbed onto my bicycle and rode up the hill to investigate.

I remembered a story Eloise Purser had told me about her older brother, Crawford, who had gone to the Mansion one night on a dare from his friends. When he walked into the darkened living room, he found a head sitting on the floor in a pool of blood. He ran for the door, but it was jammed. Somebody started laughing, and for a minute Crawford thought it was the head. Of course, it was the friends who had dared him to come. The friends came out from behind a table and lit a candle, which showed that the head was a pumpkin and the blood was ketchup.

As I got off my bike and approached the house, the wind whipped around and a loose shutter next to the door began to flap, making a banging sound. A face appeared at the window. For a minute I thought of the bloody head, then I noticed that the face was wearing glasses. It was Johnny Scopes.

"Hi, kiddo," he called. He left the window and a moment later appeared in the doorway, wearing an old pair of overalls and a shirt that was spattered with paint. Even so, he was the handsomest man I had ever seen.

"I thought you were home in Illinois," I said.

He grinned. "I can go back if you want."

"No, no, please. I'm just surprised. But it's a nice surprise. What brought you back?"

"When the trial date got changed, I figured I'd better come down and help folks get ready. Come in and see what we're doing."

He stepped aside, and I walked past him into the parlor. My arm brushed against his. Where we touched, I got a warm, tingly feeling.

I looked around. The last time I'd been in the room it had been dingy, with cobwebs hanging from the ceiling. Now the cobwebs were gone, and the walls had been freshly painted. The only thing left to paint was the trim, which was what Johnny had been working on when I arrived. There was a drop cloth spread out along one wall, with a paint can and brush resting on it.

As I looked around, George Rappleyea entered the room, wearing work clothes and carrying a wrench.

"Welcome to defense headquarters," he said, shifting from foot to foot. He was always fidgeting, like someone waiting for a bus.

I said, "Is this for the trial?"

Rappleyea nodded. "I thought that with all the visitors in town, anyone in favor of evolution might have a hard time finding a room. My company owns this place, so I decided the defense lawyers could stay here. It needed fixing up, though."

Johnny moved to the wall and flipped a switch. Above my head a chandelier lit up. "We've redone the wiring and fixed all the lights, so I'm afraid Halloween may not be as much fun this year."

Rappleyea said, "I've been working on the plumbing. The hall bathroom is giving me fits. I'd better get back to it." Twitching, he hurried off.

Johnny walked over to the drop cloth, picked up the paintbrush, and resumed his work, humming as he did.

"What's that song?" I asked.

"'Stairway to Paradise.' George Gershwin wrote it."

"Who's he?"

Johnny stared at me. "George Gershwin's the most famous songwriter there is. My God, he wrote 'Swanee' and *Rhapsody in Blue*."

I could feel my cheeks get hot. I tried to say something smart, but all I could think of was, "Blue's my favorite color."

"It's not the color blue," he said. "It's a kind of music. Haven't you heard of the blues?"

"I guess not."

I thought of the stories I'd heard about Johnny driving to Morgan Springs and dancing to the music of a live band. It was a side of him I knew nothing about.

"I've heard of the Charleston," I said. "People around town say it's a dance you do when you go to Morgan Springs."

He laughed. "That's one rumor they got right. We do all kinds of dances—the Charleston, the turkey trot. There's even one called the monkey glide."

Johnny put down his paintbrush, stepped away from the wall, and began humming "Stairway to Paradise" again.

As he did, he moved back and forth in a smooth motion.

"That's the monkey glide," he said. "Want to try it?"

He held out his hand. I took it, and he led me around the floor, demonstrating the steps and coaching me until I got the idea.

"Hey, you're a pretty good dancer," he said.

I pictured myself in a beautiful dress, moving with Johnny across a dance floor. A band was playing songs by George Gershwin, and I knew the words to every single one. It was just Johnny and me and the music.

Then Johnny ruffled my hair, and I was back in Dayton, a fifteen-year-old kid who rode a bicycle and had smudges on her face. He picked up his paintbrush and got back to work.

I said, "The place is looking nice."

"I should hope so," he said. "A few weeks from now, Clarence Darrow himself might be staying in this house."

"Is it true what they say about him? That he doesn't believe in God?"

Johnny glanced up at me. "I wish people would stop saying that. He's an agnostic, not an atheist."

"What does that mean?"

"An atheist believes there is no God. An agnostic isn't sure."

"How can he not be sure?" I said. "I thought he was supposed to be smart."

Johnny chuckled. "You've been living in Dayton too long."

He went back to his painting, leaving me to figure out what he meant. A moment later he said, "Frances, where did you get the idea that smart people don't have doubts?"

"My father's smart, and he doesn't."

"You really think so?" asked Johnny.

"Well, yes," I said.

Johnny tilted his head, his blue eyes sparkling. "What would you say if I told you I'm an agnostic?"

"You don't believe in God? I mean, you're not sure?"

He said, "First you have to tell me which God we're talking about. If it's the one who sends people to a fiery pit for making a few mistakes, then no, I don't believe in God. If it's the one who loves us no matter what we do . . . Well, I'd like to believe in that one, I really would. I just don't see much proof."

"So, you don't believe in the Bible?"

"I believe in what it teaches. I believe in Jesus, too, and I try to lead a Christian life. I'm just not sure there's a God."

"But you go to church."

"That's where the people are," he said. "They're the ones I believe in. They may not be perfect, but they're real. I can reach out and shake their hands. That's all I would need to convince me there's a God. If he gave me one good handshake, I'd sign up in a minute."

"Daddy says there's a God, and I believe him."

"You love your father, don't you?" said Johnny.

"Yes, I do."

"I love mine, too. He stopped going to church years ago. Said he was tired of people talking one way and acting another. Said he needed a religion that had room for doubt and never did find one."

I said, "I think that's sad."

Johnny smiled. "He's one of the happiest people I know. You'll see—he's coming to Dayton for the trial."

There was the sound of rapid footsteps, and George Rappleyea appeared at the doorway, his glasses crooked and his hair sticking out on one side.

"You've got to see this," he said.

He led us down the hall and into the bathroom, where, with a flourish, he flushed the commode. "Ta-da!"

Nothing happened.

"That's funny," he said. He stepped to the sink and turned on the faucet. It was dry. Muttering to himself, Rappleyea left the bathroom and went out the back door.

"Must be the water supply," Johnny said as we followed.

Rappleyea's black sedan and Johnny's familiar yellow Dodge were parked in back. Beyond them a water pipe snaked out the rear of the house and up the hill.

Rappleyea checked the pipe, starting at the house. When he reached the back of the property, he called out, "Look at this!"

Hurrying over, we saw that two pipe sections had come apart at the joint and water was streaming down the hill. Rappleyea quickly knelt down to repair the break.

"Must have pulled loose," Johnny said.

"Pipes don't pull loose by themselves," said Rappleyea. "Somebody did this."

"You mean, on purpose?" I asked.

Rappleyea nodded. "It's sabotage," he declared.

Johnny laughed. "Come on, George, this isn't New York."

"Not much water has gathered," said Rappleyea. "It must have just happened." Studying the area around the pipe, he pointed to some rough holes in the mud. "What do you call these?"

"I don't know," Johnny said. "What do you call them?"

"Footprints," said Rappleyea. He followed the pipeline up the hill, scrambling through the bushes, looking left and right. A few minutes later he was back. I noticed that he was blinking a lot, and his fidgeting had grown worse.

Johnny said, "I think you've been working too hard. Let's take a break, and I'll buy you a Coca-Cola."

He loaded my bicycle into his Dodge and the three of us got in. As we drove off, I glanced back at the Mansion. I couldn't help but remember that when I'd looked up from Mrs. Cate's house and seen something moving, it had been in the backyard.

EIGHT

The next morning I woke up thinking about the water pipe at the Mansion. Suddenly I wasn't tired anymore. I scrambled out of bed, pulled on some clothes, and hurried across the street to see Eloise. She was sitting on her front porch swing, reading a mystery book.

"You want to investigate a real mystery?" I asked.

Her eyes lit up. "Sure!"

"Come on."

We hopped on our bikes, and I led the way up to the Mansion. The place was closed, so we went to the back, where I showed Eloise the water pipe and told her what had happened. In the mud around the pipe were the flat, round holes we had seen the day before.

Eloise bent down and examined the holes. "You really think these are footprints?"

"Mr. Rappleyea says they are."

She got a funny look on her face. "You mean that man from New York?"

"He's really not so bad," I said.

"These don't look like footprints to me."

I checked the ground in a wider area, and something caught my eye. "Look at this," I said.

Eloise came over, and I showed her a footprint, outlined clearly in dried mud.

"It's a strange kind of shoe," I said. "The sole isn't smooth. It looks like a waffle iron."

"It's a boot," she said. "The kind that workers wear. Did you see anyone wearing boots here yesterday?"

I shook my head. "Mr. Rappleyea had on some old shoes. Johnny did too. I noticed Johnny's because they were splattered with paint."

Eloise said, "You know, this footprint could have been left by another worker. It doesn't prove anything."

"What about the broken pipe?" I said.

"Accidents happen."

"Yes," I said, "but this one happened where Clarence Darrow will be staying. People around here think he's against God, the Bible, and just about everything else they believe in."

"What are you saying?" she asked.

"I think someone broke the pipe on purpose, to make trouble for Darrow and Johnny's lawyers."

She said, "You think anyone in Dayton would do that?"

"Eloise, Dayton isn't paradise. No town is. People want to get their way. They'll do things to get it, like break a pipe, or worse."

"I don't believe that."

I said, "Don't you ever wonder about things? Maybe everything our parents told us is true. But maybe it's not. Johnny Scopes is a wonderful man, and he doesn't believe in God. He could be right. Our parents could be wrong."

"Will you stop saying that?"

"Look at those mountains," I said. "Did you ever think about what's on the other side? There's Atlanta. There's Chicago and New York. Not to mention places like Paris and Tokyo and Bombay. You think everybody there believes what we do? Who's to say that we're right and they're wrong?"

Eloise glared at me. "Why do you have to make everything so complicated? God made the world in seven days. Jesus loves me. I love my parents. I believe what they tell me. And I think the broken pipe was an accident."

She went to her bike and climbed on. "I'm going back. Are you coming?"

"I guess so," I said. "I didn't mean to get you all upset. I've just been thinking about things, that's all."

"You think too much," said Eloise, and started off down the hill.

I looked back at the pipe and studied it for a minute. Then I sighed, got on my bike, and followed Eloise back into town.

I was still thinking about the water pipe when I went to the store later that day. I found Daddy and Sue Hicks on ladders outside, hanging a banner from a couple of big oak trees in front.

"How does it look?" Daddy called to me.

"Higher on the left," I said. "Higher, higher . . . there, that's good."

Sue leaned back to look at the words.

ROBINSON'S DRUG STORE
WHERE IT STARTED

"I guess nobody has to ask what *it* is," he said, chuckling.

Daddy said, "If they do, we haven't done our job with publicity."

They climbed down, and I helped them put the ladders away. As the two of them went inside, I looked up to see Johnny Scopes approaching in his yellow roadster. I smoothed my skirt and tried to put on my most charming smile.

Johnny parked the car and vaulted over the door, barely even noticing me. He headed for the store like a man on a mission.

"Johnny?" I said.

"Huh? Oh, hi, Frances."

"There's something I want to tell you."

He glanced from me to the store and back again. "Sure, what is it?"

"Eloise and I went to the Mansion. We saw another

footprint." I described the print and where we'd found it, but he didn't seem to be listening.

"Thanks for telling me, kiddo," he said. He went into the store, and I followed.

Sue Hicks had just settled in with a Coca-Cola when he saw Johnny. "Look, everybody, it's the jailbird."

"He's not a jailbird," I said.

"He broke the law, didn't he?" said Sue.

Johnny glared at him. "This trial wasn't my idea, you know. You're the ones who asked me to do it."

Sue grinned. "You're gonna lose, boy."

As I watched Sue, I thought of the footprint and wondered if he owned a pair of boots.

Daddy, who had been making Coca-Colas with Sonny, stepped out from behind the soda fountain. "Now, let's calm down," he said. "We're all on the same side here."

"Tell him that," said Johnny.

There was an uncomfortable silence. Sue gazed at Johnny, then reached for his Coca-Cola and downed it in one gulp. "Gentlemen, I need to get back to my office."

"I thought this was your office," said Sonny.

Suddenly Daddy was overcome by a fit of coughing. Sue shook his head and left. Johnny watched him go, then turned to Daddy. "Mr. Earle, if you have a minute I'd like to talk to you, please. In private."

Daddy put his arm around Johnny's shoulders and led

him to the back of the store. They lowered their voices, but I could still make out the words.

"What's on your mind, son?" asked Daddy.

Johnny said, "I asked Mr. White about my teaching contract for the fall. He said I should talk to you."

"It's a little early for contracts, isn't it? School won't start for two and a half months."

"Jane Beasley got hers," said Johnny. "So did Michael Pratt."

"I'd say your situation's a little different. Let's just wait and see what happens, shall we?"

"Mr. Earle, you said this trial wouldn't affect my job."

"It'll be fine, son," said Daddy. "It'll be fine, don't you worry."

Johnny nodded. When he left, I couldn't help but notice two things. He didn't say good-bye to me. And he did look worried.

As for Daddy, he was smiling, as usual. But there was a tightness around his mouth and a look in his eyes that I hadn't seen before. It was harder, sterner, like a glimpse of someone I didn't know.

NINE

Over the next few weeks Daddy spent most of his time getting ready for the trial, and we didn't see much of him at home. Mama joked that she'd been replaced by a monkey, but I knew that behind the smile she really was upset. Sometimes Daddy wouldn't come home until late at night, and through the bedroom wall I'd hear Mama accuse him of neglecting his family. His answer was always the same: This was his chance to put Dayton on the map and he wasn't going to miss it.

Eloise and I didn't want to miss it either. We roamed the streets, watching the preparations, while I stayed alert for signs of sabotage and mischief.

We saw banners all over town that said READ YOUR BIBLE, including one right outside the courthouse. We visited Mr. Darwin—not Charles Darwin but J. R. Darwin, who owned a clothing store on Market Street. Sometime in June, J. R. decided that Charles was a distant cousin, and we helped him hang a sign outside his store.

DARWIN IS RIGHT
INSIDE

We noticed that next door to Robinson's, the Aqua Hotel was gearing up for business. They filled several of their rooms with cots and even put some in the hallways. Another hotel, the Dayton, had been closed for years, but Walter Nixon leased the place and began fixing it up. With the help of his two boys, Wilfred and Howard, he also set up a lemonade stand on Main Street. I'm proud to say that Eloise and I were their first customers.

The Morgan Springs Hotel, where Johnny went dancing on Saturday nights, expanded their schedule for the trial, announcing that they would have a live jazz orchestra playing every night.

New telephone and telegraph lines were strung, and Western Union made plans to send twenty more operators to Dayton for the trial. A big storage area above Bailey's Hardware was converted into a pressroom for reporters. The telephone company and post office hired extra workers.

There had been talk about where to hold the trial. Since the Rhea County Courthouse would be too small for the crowd, some folks thought a new grandstand should be built for the ballpark so the trial could be held there. They even talked about selling tickets. But the state attorney general's office got wind of the plan and put an end to it, saying that the courthouse, one of the largest in the state, would do just fine. I heard that Judge Raulston was disappointed, because he had plans to buy a big batch of tickets for his friends and relatives.

Once the courthouse was selected, workers started fixing it up. They gave the walls a fresh coat of paint and added extra seats. Outside they set up a wooden speaker's platform on the lawn. To make sure everybody would be comfortable, a row of outhouses was built in back of the courthouse.

One day in early July, Eloise and I were sitting on her front porch with her brother, Crawford, when a big truck pulled up to the courthouse with the words "Chicago Tribune" painted on the side. We hurried over to watch as a crew of workers climbed out and began unloading equipment.

When I asked one of the workers what they were doing, he grinned and said, "Little lady, we're wiring this place for sound."

They set up twenty loudspeakers on the courthouse lawn and another four or five in auditoriums around town. Then they put three microphones at the front of the courtroom: one for the lawn, one for the auditoriums, and one more with the letters *WGN* on it.

"What does that mean?" Crawford asked the worker.

"It means this place is going to be famous," he said. "We'll be doing radio broadcasts from the courtroom."

When the Chicago workers finished setting up

microphones, another group arrived from Western Union. We watched as they strung wires into the courtroom, where a telegraph operator would be tapping out up-to-the-minute reports. Besides telegraph and radio, there also would be movie cameras. A platform was built at the back of the courtroom where newsreel photographers could stand, taking moving pictures that would be shown all over the world.

A few days later the people started to arrive. I know because I served most of them at our soda fountain, where they were driven by weather that was hot even for Dayton. There was a thermometer outside, and when Daddy and I opened the store we would check the temperature. That summer it was rarely lower than ninety degrees, even at eight in the morning. Daddy loved it. He called it Coca-Cola weather.

The reporters were the first to come. There were more than two hundred of them, from places as far away as London, England. They would poke around town, interviewing people and taking pictures. Eventually they wound up at Robinson's, where they would try to get free food in exchange for publicity. Daddy just grinned and said he was getting all the publicity he needed.

The preachers came too—every kind from Holy Rollers to Foot-Washing Baptists. A lot of them weren't official preachers at all. They were just folks who talked to God on a regular basis, and he had told them to head for Dayton. They set up on street corners around town, preaching at the top of their lungs to anybody who would listen.

One called himself Bible Champion of the World. Another was John the Baptist the Third. Still another claimed to be Absolute Ruler of the Entire World, Without Military, Naval, or Other Physical Force.

An enormous man with a straw hat and rings of perspiration under his arms set up outside Robinson's, proclaiming that Clarence Darrow was the beast described in the book of Revelation, with seven heads and ten horns. As he spoke, a man drove by, shouting through a megaphone, "The life of Christ—the greatest movie of all time!" On the side of his car were signs lit up with electric lightbulbs:

COME SEE IT!

THE CRUCIFIXION, THE ASCENSION, THE RESURRECTION, AND MANY OTHER INCIDENTS! ˙

The courthouse lawn took on the appearance of an open-air bazaar, with rows of wooden stalls where you could buy anything from hot dogs to souvenir key rings. Down the street were two tent shows: *The She Devil* and *Suwanee River: A Romance of the Old South.* Musicians were everywhere, including an old blind man who had written a song for the occasion:

We read of a place called heaven
It's made for the pure and the free
These truths in God's words he hath given
How beautiful heaven must be!

One of the visitors was shorter and hairier than the rest. His name was Joe Mendi, and he was a chimpanzee. Joe Mendi dressed like a man, wearing a tuxedo and bow tie. He was accompanied by his trainer, a woman, and wherever the two of them went they were followed by crowds of people, mostly children. Naturally they ended up at Robinson's, where a photographer took a picture of them sitting at a table with Daddy, Sonny, and me. The picture shows Joe Mendi doing what everyone else did at Robinson's. He was drinking a Coca-Cola.

What the picture didn't show was what happened next. Mama, who had never been fond of animals and was developing a particular dislike of monkeys, noticed what Joe Mendi was doing and let out a shriek. She grabbed his glass and, holding it at arm's length the way you might carry a live snake, hurried to the sink and poured out the Coca-Cola. Then she dropped the glass into a paper bag, set the bag on the floor, and stomped on it, to make sure no one had to drink from a glass that had been used by a monkey.

Most years the Fourth of July was an important event in Dayton. There was a parade, the mayor would give a speech, and afterward people would gather for a picnic and contests. Prizes were given for the the oldest person, the youngest baby, and the best pie. One year Eloise and I won a ribbon in the three-legged race.

My favorite part was the fireworks. In the evening Mama would make fried chicken and potato salad, which we ate on our big front porch. Then, when it got dark, a crowd would gather across the street on the courthouse lawn. We would turn off the porch light, and Mr. Culpepper, the safety director, would set up in front of the courthouse and shoot off fireworks. Daddy would give American flags to Sonny and me, and we would wave them at the sky to celebrate our freedom.

The funny thing was, that year people barely noticed the Fourth of July. There was no parade, no contests, no fireworks. My family had dinner on the front porch, and Daddy handed out flags, just like always, but there was nothing to wave them at. Sonny lit up a sparkler, but it fizzled out. Finally we set the flags aside, where they hung limp in the hot, dead air.

TEN

I began to notice that several times a day Daddy would slip to the back of the store and spend time hunched over his rolltop desk. Whenever anyone approached, he would pull out his ledger sheet and pretend to be looking at sales. I sneaked to the desk once when he was gone and looked through his papers but didn't find anything. One time I even asked him what he was doing back there. He just got a mysterious look on his face and turned away.

Three days before the trial began, I was helping him with some window displays when a truck pulled up in front of the store. The door opened, and out stepped old Mr. Davis, the printer. Daddy stopped what he was doing and hurried out to meet him. I decided to go along.

"Mornin', Mr. Earle," said Mr. Davis. "Got something for you."

He opened the back of the truck, and inside were ten big boxes. Opening a pocketknife, he slit open one of the boxes, pulled out a small flat booklet, and handed it to Daddy.

"What is it?" I asked.

Daddy didn't answer. He studied the cover, running his fingers across it, then opened the booklet and slowly leafed through the pages. When he finished, he leaned down and handed it to me.

"This is a little present from your Daddy. Save it and show it to your children someday."

On the front of the booklet were the words "Why Dayton—Of All Places?" Inside was information about the town and how it came to host the greatest trial of the century.

"Who wrote this?" I asked.

"Yours truly," he said. "Why do you think I've been spending so much time at my desk?" He grinned. "Didn't know your old man was an author, did you?"

It was a handsome booklet. I wanted to give Daddy a hug and say I was proud of him. But I found myself wondering what Johnny Scopes would think about it. He might say that Daddy had paid for the printing of the booklets, but Johnny had paid too, and might keep paying for a long time.

Mr. Davis said, "You want to give me a hand with these boxes?"

"No problem," said Daddy. He stepped inside the store and called Billy Langford. Together Daddy and Billy lifted the boxes from the truck and carried them to the stockroom. When they finished, Mr. Davis latched the tailgate and climbed back into the truck.

"Let me get my checkbook," said Daddy.

Mr. Davis waved him off. "You're good for it," he said. "I'll send you a bill." He backed out into the street and drove away.

Daddy turned to Billy and me. "Come on, we've got work to do."

We finished the window displays, then set up a rack for the booklets at the front of the store. Daddy made up a sign that said TRIAL SOUVENIRS—5¢ and hung it above the rack. Then we loaded the rack with booklets, leaving the rest in the stockroom.

As we finished, Eloise hurried into the store, shouting, "He's here! Mr. Bryan's here!"

"Where?" I asked.

"At the station. His train is coming in right now."

"Hooray!" cried Sonny. "Who's Mr. Bryan?"

I turned to Daddy. "Can I go? Please?"

Daddy thought for a minute. "Two conditions," he said. "Number one, take Sonny with you."

"Hooray!" said Sonny.

"And number two, put some of these booklets in a bag. Maybe you can sell a few."

By the time we arrived at the station, a big crowd had gathered, including at least fifty reporters and photographers. The train had just pulled in, and the crowd was surging up and down the length of the train, looking for the man they called the Great Commoner. Finally, in the doorway of the last car, a head appeared.

"There he is!" someone shouted.

The man stepped off the train wearing a black coat and bow tie. He was tall, with stooped shoulders, a pointed nose, and a chin jutting out from beneath his hat. He took off the hat to reveal a bald head with gray hair on the sides. He looked older than I had expected—older even than my Grandpa Haggard, who I always thought was about as old as you could get.

The reporters had their notebooks out, firing questions at him. Eloise, Sonny, and I moved to the front so we could see. Bryan raised his hand, and immediately the crowd got quiet. I imagined he must have looked something like Moses did when he brought the Ten Commandments down from Mount Sinai.

"Just say that I am here," Bryan told the reporters, his voice ringing out like the chimes at First Methodist Church. "I am going right to work, and I am ready for anything that is to be done."

With that, the prosecution lawyers moved in around him, led by Sue Hicks, so the photographers could get some pictures. When they were finished, Bryan turned to the crowd and waved. As he did, Sonny tugged at his coat.

Bryan crouched down and shook Sonny's hand. "Young man, what's your name?"

"Sonny Robinson. This is my sister, Frances. My father runs the drug store."

Bryan smiled. "Well, Sonny, I'm sure your father's a fine

man. And he's lucky to have such a nice son and daughter."

Thinking about Daddy, suddenly I knew what he would do in that situation. I reached into my bag and pulled out one of the booklets.

"This is for you, Mr. Bryan, compliments of Robinson's Drugs," I said. "Drop in anytime and we'll serve you a refreshing drink called a Monkey Fizz."

Grinning, Bryan took the booklet. "A Monkey Fizz, huh? Thank you, Frances, I'll be sure to do that."

One of the reporters said, "Could I have one of those booklets?"

"You surely may," I replied. "That'll be a nickel."

He paid me, and a dozen other people lined up behind him. Before I knew it, the booklets were gone.

Bryan, meanwhile, was taken to a waiting car and shook hands all the way. One man gave him a bag of radishes. I was surprised to see Bryan open the bag right there and bite into a radish as if it were a fat red apple. By the time he reached the car, the radish was gone and he was working on another one.

Bryan was driven down Market Street, past crowds of cheering people, to the home of F. R. Rogers, where he and his wife would be staying. He changed clothes and walked around town, followed by reporters and well-wishers wherever he went. True to his word, he ended up at Robinson's. Daddy came out front and shook his hand.

"I'm happy to meet you," said Bryan, "but to tell you the truth I came to see your daughter." As Daddy stared,

Bryan turned to me and smiled warmly. "It's good to see you again, Frances."

I curtsied and said, "Thank you, Mr. Bryan. Won't you come in?"

I offered him my arm, and together we went inside. Daddy followed, along with half the people in town, or at least as many as could fit into the store. The rest milled around outside, talking among themselves and trying to peer in through the display windows.

I showed Bryan to a table and brought him a Monkey Fizz, just as I'd promised. Taking a gulp, he pronounced it delicious. He was still holding the bag of radishes and bit into another one between sips of the drink. He asked for a menu and to my amazement ordered two ham specials, potato salad, and a strawberry sundae.

While Bryan ate, Billy Langford and I took orders at the soda fountain, and Sonny delivered them to the tables. Daddy set up shop at the front of the store, selling booklets as quickly as he could unpack them.

A half hour later Bryan finished the last of his strawberry sundae.

"Would you like anything else?" I asked when he was done.

"No, thank you, dear," he said. "I'm on a special diet."

The way people in Dayton talked about Clarence Darrow, I expected him to charge into town breathing fire. But the man who got off the train the next day was old and rumpled, with a large nose and wispy brown hair. He was shorter than Bryan but had wide shoulders and big hands. His voice, like his skin, was rough and leathery.

Johnny Scopes, who had brought me to the station with him, shook Darrow's hand and said, "I'm glad to see you, sir."

It was another hot day, and Darrow had taken off his jacket, revealing a pair of red suspenders. Glancing at some of the other Dayton residents who had come to meet him, Darrow said to Johnny, "I see that down here you wear suspenders too."

"Yes, sir, we do."

Darrow said, "I'm glad to hear it. So, in spite of what Mr. Bryan might want, the law of gravity hasn't been repealed yet."

The reporters clustered around, and one of them, a young woman, asked Darrow if he believed in God.

Sensing a trap, he said, "What is God, ma'am?"

"Well, I suppose God is love."

He gazed at the woman thoughtfully for a moment. "God is love," he said. "Yes, then, I believe in God."

There were more questions, then Johnny loaded Darrow's bags into his car and the two of us drove him up to the Mansion. We talked on the way, and the more I heard Darrow, with his gravelly voice and colorful stories, the more he reminded me of men I knew in Dayton.

When we arrived at the Mansion, we found the front door open.

"That's strange," said Johnny. "George Rappleyea told me the place would be locked up."

He hopped out of the car to investigate. Darrow and I followed. As we walked through the open door, a dark shape bounded into the hallway. It had a strange, hunched-over appearance and was breathing hard. Grunting, the shape moved forward, heading straight for us. Johnny flinched. I screamed.

Two more figures appeared at the end of the hall. The first stepped into the light, and we saw that it was a woman with long black hair and a stern face. She snapped her fingers, and the shape immediately halted. It turned and leaped into her arms.

"Bad boy, Joe Mendi!" she said. "Bad boy!"

The dark shape was Joe Mendi the chimpanzee, wearing shoes, pants, a coat, and tie. The woman was his trainer. Behind her was a stout man with long white hair.

The man said, "Pardon us, gentlemen. We were just inspecting the premises when Joe Mendi decided to do some exploring of his own."

"How did you get inside?" asked Johnny.

"The door was open," said the man. "We walked right in. We heard some noise in back, but no one was there."

Recognizing Darrow, the man pushed his way past Johnny and held out his hand. "Mr. Darrow, permit me to introduce myself. My name is Harry Beckenstahl. I'm the owner of Joe Mendi, the most amazing, most remarkable, most manlike monkey on the face of the earth."

"You sound like some lawyers I know," said Darrow.

"No, sir," said Beckenstahl, "I'm with the circus."

"Same thing," Darrow grunted.

Beckenstahl said, "We didn't mean to frighten you. We simply wanted to offer the services of Joe Mendi to the defense team."

"Is he a Baptist?" asked Darrow.

"No," said Beckenstahl, not cracking a smile, "but in most other ways he's almost human—his clothes, manners, eating habits. Don't you see, gentlemen? Joe Mendi demonstrates beyond the shadow of a doubt that people descended from monkeys. He's living proof of evolution."

Darrow said, "It's a tempting offer, Mr. Beckenstahl, but I'm afraid we'll have to decline."

"Oh?" said Beckenstahl. "Mind if I ask why?"

"Out of respect to our colleagues on the prosecution," Darrow said. "If we put Joe Mendi on the witness stand, they might look bad by comparison."

Johnny had more practical things on his mind. "I hope your monkey didn't mess up the house. We just cleaned it this morning."

Beckenstahl sniffed. "You didn't do a very good job. The place is a mess."

It was true. As we went from room to room, we saw

overturned tables, disheveled beds, and drawers dumped out on the floor. With each new discovery Johnny became more upset.

"Someone in town did this," he said. "They must have broken in."

"You really think so?" I asked.

His eyes were bright and angry, and his face was red. "They're ganging up on me, Frances. They want to win this trial, no matter what it takes."

Toward the rear of the house the damage stopped. We found the back door wide open. Johnny said, "They must have been here when Beckenstahl arrived. It looks like he interrupted them."

"Maybe they were looking for something," I said.

"Maybe," said Johnny. "More likely, they were trying to intimidate us."

Darrow chuckled. "They'll have to do better than this. I get death threats every day along with the morning paper."

"Welcome to Dayton, Mr. Darrow," said Johnny. "Land of the free, home of the brave. They treat you fine, as long as you do what they say and read your Bible."

Harry Beckenstahl gave Darrow his card and left, taking Joe Mendi and the trainer with him. I helped Johnny straighten up the place and get Darrow settled, then Johnny drove me home.

In the car I said, "Remember the footprints in back of

the Mansion? Maybe those same people are the ones who broke in."

I could see that Johnny was still upset. "I was thinking the same thing," he said.

It was a warm night. With the car top down, the breeze felt good. I said, "I heard you and Daddy talking at the store the other day. You know, about your contract."

Johnny looked surprised. "That's grown-up business, Frances."

"I'm fifteen years old. I'm almost grown-up." He didn't say anything, so I went on. "I don't think it's fair, what they're doing to you. Daddy said the trial wouldn't affect your job, and now they're holding back your contract."

"Your father's a good man," said Johnny. "I'm sure we'll be able to work it out."

"Sometimes I wonder if I really know him," I said. "He gets this hard, cold look on his face. Like that day in the store. And I've noticed he doesn't always tell the truth. He doesn't lie exactly. He just uses the part he likes and throws away the rest, the way you'd do with an apple or a watermelon."

"Don't you think everyone does that?" asked Johnny.

"Maybe a little bit. But he does it all the time. He picks out the part he likes, tells people about it, and calls it publicity."

Johnny frowned. The trial was Daddy's biggest publicity

scheme, and Johnny was one of the parts he was using.

Johnny said, "Do you believe in evolution?"

"What does that have to do with it?"

"Evolution is change. That's what it means. Animals change. People change. Beliefs change too. It might be nice if you could go to a book that had everything written down in black and white and it stayed the same forever. But when I look around, that's not the world I see. I see everything changing. Personally, I think that makes it more interesting, don't you?"

"I don't want my father to change," I said.

"I wasn't talking about him," said Johnny. "I was talking about you."

I looked over at him. He was watching the road, his hair blowing in the breeze. "What about love?" I said. "Does that change?"

He thought for a moment, then said, "I think it changes shape and size. Maybe it changes names. But love itself? No, I don't think it changes."

"I don't either," I said, gazing at him. "At least, I hope it doesn't."

When we arrived at my house, Johnny pulled up in front. I got out and closed the door. He smiled at me, then waved and drove away, his red taillights disappearing into the night.

ELEVEN

Johnny! It's great to see you, lad."

An older, shorter version of Johnny Scopes bounded off the train and gave his son a hug. He had a big red mustache and a pipe, but otherwise I could have been looking at Johnny in thirty years.

Thomas Scopes had traveled from Illinois that morning. I'd been eager to meet him, so Johnny had agreed to let me come along to Chattanooga to meet the train.

Johnny introduced us, then his father shook Johnny's hand and slapped him on the back. "So, lad, how are they treating you?" he asked.

I noticed he spoke with an accent and remembered that Johnny had once told me his father was born in England.

"Just fine, Pop," said Johnny. "Truth is, there's not much to do right now. I've been helping around town in the mornings, then going down to the creek most afternoons."

"What are you helping with?" asked Mr. Scopes.

"He does just about everything," I said. "Driving people around, carrying their bags . . ."

Mr. Scopes laughed. "Carrying their bags? Laddie boy, you're the star of the show. They should be carrying your bags!"

"Aw, Pop, it's not like that," said Johnny, looking pained.

Mr. Scopes squeezed his shoulder. "You know I'm just teasing. I'm proud of you, lad, and eager to see this town of yours. Now, would you get my bags, please?"

When we returned to Dayton, the place was overflowing with people, laughing, arguing, shaking their fists, and praising God. With the trial due to start the next day, thousands of new arrivals were on hand, and it seemed that all of them were standing in the road, blocking our way. Johnny inched along Market Street, honking his horn and shouting, but people barely noticed.

Mr. Scopes winked at me and said, "So, Johnny, is this what it's like in your classroom?"

With all the activity, I asked Johnny to drop me off at the courthouse square so I could look around. He was about to pull over and let me out when suddenly there was a thump, and the car lurched to a stop. Johnny leaped from the car to investigate. Mr. Scopes and I scrambled out right behind him.

Sprawled on the ground in front of the car was a short, squat man with a large head, a barrel chest, and a cigar dangling from his mouth. The man had shaggy eyebrows and bright eyes, and he wore a necktie, in spite of the fact that he appeared to have no neck.

"Are you all right, sir?" asked Johnny, offering his hand.

The man waved him off, then climbed to his feet, saying, "Believe me, kid, I've been hit by cars a lot better than yours." Puffing his cigar, he strolled over to a couple of friends who were standing nearby. "First they try to save your soul, then they run you over. Frankly, I'm not sure which is worse."

Something about the way he said it made me mad. "We were barely moving," I told him. "Besides, you were standing in the middle of the street. That's illegal."

The man cocked one eyebrow and gazed down at me. "Just what we need—another lawyer. This place has more lawyers than flies, which is saying a lot."

His friends laughed, and the three of them moved off into the crowd.

"We're blocking traffic, lad," said Mr. Scopes, and they climbed back into the car.

"Thanks for the ride," I told them. "I'm going to look around. It was nice meeting you, Mr. Scopes."

I followed the crowd onto the courthouse lawn. In spite of all the people around, jostling and shoving and carrying on, I hardly recognized anyone. It appeared that most of Dayton had migrated to the mountains, leaving the town to strangers. There were farm families with squalling babies, hawkers selling patent medicine, barefoot children playing hide-and-seek, mountain men with coon dogs and squirrel guns, and reporters everywhere, scribbling notes and taking pictures of it all.

"I'll take one of those monkeys," said a familiar voice behind me.

Turning around, I saw the man with the cigar buying a stuffed monkey. He held the monkey up to his friends, pretending to make it talk.

"Hi, you-all," he said with a phony Southern accent. "Welcome to mah hometown of Dayton, Tennessee." His friends roared their approval, and the man said, "Don't laugh. This monkey used to be mayor."

Tucking the monkey under his arm, the man set out through the crowd, stopping occasionally to chat with this person or that and making sly comments to his friends, who seemed to think the whole thing was hilarious. I didn't think it was funny at all, but I found myself following.

The man moved around to the side of the courthouse, where suddenly he was confronted by a stocky preacher with bright red cheeks and gray hair that stuck out in all directions. Sweat poured from the preacher's forehead, running down his stiff collar and onto his long black coat, which he swept around him like a cape.

"Greetings in the name of the Lord!" boomed the preacher, pumping the man's hand as if trying to draw a bucket of water. "Reverend T. T. Martin, field secretary of the Anti-Evolution League. Here's a little pamphlet I wrote myself, called 'Hell in the High Schools.'"

The man scanned the pamphlet, puffing thoughtfully on his cigar. "Reverend Martin—"

"Please, call me T. T."

"T. T.," said the man, "I have just one question: Do you really believe this hogwash?"

Martin smiled. "Sir, I'd stake my life on it."

"Does this mean that if I believe in evolution, I'm going to hell?"

"Absolutely," said Martin. "Nothing personal, of course."

"Good," said the man. "I've got a hunch they have more fun down there than in the other place."

Martin threw back his head and laughed. "Touché, sir, touché! You have no idea how happy this makes me."

"It does?" said the man.

"I've been looking all day for an evolutionist to convert," said Martin. "I can save these other folks with one hand tied behind my back."

Grinning, the man crossed his arms and rocked back on his heels. "Well, then, fire away," he said.

Martin glanced around, and his gaze came to rest on me. "Look at this sweet girl here," he said. "Do you honestly believe she descended from apes?"

The man held his stuffed monkey next to my face. "There's a family resemblance, don't you think?"

I heard laughter and saw the man's friends standing nearby. Furious, not knowing what else to do, I stuck my tongue out at them.

"There, you see?" said the man. "I rest my case."

Blushing, I quickly pulled my tongue back in. But Martin wasn't giving up.

"Young lady," he said, "stick out that tongue again, please."

I did as he asked, puzzled and a little embarrassed.

Martin said, "Sir, the theory of evolution can be disproved using the smallest detail of God's creation, including this tongue. Observe how it can be made long and round, or wide and flat, or curled like the petal of an orchid. Show him, child. See that? And look at all these thousands of tiny taste buds. Some are for sweet, some for sour, some salty, some bitter. It's a miracle of creation, and it's just a tongue! Look at her nose, her lips, her eyes—my God, the windows of the soul!"

Warming to his task, Martin leaned so close that I heard him wheeze and smelled the remnants of his lunch, which apparently had included pickles and onions. He grasped my hands and held them up toward the man with the cigar.

"Fingers! Look at 'em! Not nine, not eleven, but ten! Ten beautiful, perfectly formed fingers!"

I had a hangnail, but I decided not to say anything.

"And look here," said Martin. "Toes! Take off your shoes and socks, dear."

"All right, I admit she's got all the usual body parts," said the man. "What's your point?"

Martin swirled his cape around my head. "This tongue, this nose, these lips, eyes, fingers—do you honestly believe all these wonderful contrivances happened simply by accident? By pure, random chance?"

The man puffed thoughtfully on his cigar. "I admit that on the surface it seems unlikely," he said. "But the laws of chance are powerful. True, none of this could happen over a month or a year. But give me a hundred million years? By all means, sir, I'll give you an eye that will take your breath away!"

Martin chuckled. "You're very good."

"Thank you."

"Of course," said Martin, "you're still going to hell."

"I'm counting on it," the man said. "Which reminds me, is there someplace around here where I can buy a bottle of whiskey?"

"You're talking to the wrong man," said Martin. "I gave that up twenty years ago when I found the Lord."

"Pity. I wouldn't mind hoisting a few with you."

Martin grinned. "I'm sure we'll see each other again, sir. After all, I love a challenge!" He gave a courtly bow and set off through the crowd.

The man watched him go, then tucked the monkey under his arm and strolled off in the other direction. One of his friends followed, but the other, a young man about the age of Johnny Scopes, stayed behind. He was sitting on the ground with his knees crossed, hunched over a notepad. I moved around behind him and peered over his shoulder to see what he was doing.

Staring out at me from the notepad was the face of T. T. Martin. It was just a pencil sketch, but Martin looked so real that I could almost smell the pickles on his breath.

"How did you do that?" I asked.

The young man turned around. "Oh, hello." He held the sketch at arm's length and gazed at it. "How did I do it? I have no idea. I just pick up a pencil, and pictures come out the other end. It's been that way ever since I was a kid."

"Are you an artist?" I said.

"Not exactly. I draw political cartoons for the *Baltimore Sun*. My name is Edmund Duffy. If you'd like, you can call me Ed."

"I'm Frances Robinson." I held out my hand, and Edmund Duffy shook it.

"Pleased to meet you, Frances."

"They pay you to draw cartoons?" I said.

Ed grinned. "Isn't it great? I started working there last year, and I still can hardly believe it."

"Could I see some of your other ones?"

He said, "We just got here today, so I don't have much." Turning the pages of his notepad, he showed me a sketch of William Jennings Bryan and another one of Judge Raulston. As I gazed at the cartoons, I decided they weren't exactly realistic. Features were exaggerated—a nose, a chin, a balding head—but somehow those very features made the drawings more lifelike than any photo.

"They're called caricatures," he said. "If they're done

right, they tell you more about a person than any photo could." He turned another page, and there was a sketch of the man with the cigar.

"I hate him," I said.

For some reason Ed thought that was funny. "Join the club," he said, laughing. "It's got a big membership."

"Who is he?" I asked.

He looked at me, amazed. "You don't know?"

"I just met him!"

"That man is hated by people far and wide. He's the most famous newspaperman in the country, and he's here to show the world that Dayton, Tennessee, is populated by fanatics, half-wits, and monkeys."

"What's his name?" I asked.

"H. L. Mencken, of course."

PART TWO

THE TRIAL

The trial of the infidel Scopes, beginning here this hot, lovely morning, will greatly resemble, I suspect, the trial of a prohibition agent accused of mayhem in Union Hill, N.J. That is to say, it will be conducted with the most austere regard for the highest principles of jurisprudence. Judge and jury will go to extreme lengths to assure the prisoner the last and least of his rights. He will be protected in his person and feelings by the full military and naval power of the State of Tennessee. No one will be permitted to pull his nose, to pray publicly for his condemnation or even to make a face at him. But all the same he will be bumped off inevitably when the time comes, and to the applause of all right-thinking men.

—H. L. Mencken
The Baltimore Evening Sun
July 10, 1925

TWELVE

"**E**loise, over here!" I called.

I waved, and Eloise slowly made her way across the crowded courtroom. It was the first day of the trial, and people were jammed together like worms in a bucket. Finding a seat was impossible, unless you happened to know the father of the defendant.

Eloise finally reached us, and I introduced her to Mr. Scopes. He smiled. "I was saving this seat in case I made a friend. Now I've got two."

The chair was a little cramped for the two of us, but I wasn't about to complain. I'd been working since eight o'clock that morning. Daddy had sent me to the courthouse with a Radio Flyer wagon full of his booklets to sell, plus a stack of fans he had gotten from a toothpaste salesman. On the front of the fans was the message DO YOUR GUMS BLEED? Below that were the name of the toothpaste and the words "Available at Robinson's Drugs." I had set up a sign on the courthouse lawn, and an hour later I had sold everything, except for a few fans that I kept for myself. I handed one to Eloise.

"Take this," I said. "You're going to need it."

Eloise fanned herself and looked around. The courtroom was big, taking up most of the building's second floor. Windows lined three of the four walls, and that morning all of them had been opened in a hopeless attempt to attract a cool breeze.

At the front of the room was a low rectangular platform with a wooden rail around it. In the middle of the platform was the judge's bench, which I thought looked a lot like the pulpit at First Methodist Church. On either side of the bench was a flagpole, where the American and Tennessee flags hung limply in the sweltering air. The witness's chair was next to the bench, and facing that were tables, one for the prosecution lawyers and one for the defense. Along one side of the platform were chairs for the jury.

Outside the railing enough chairs had been set up for four hundred people, and another two hundred or so stood along the walls. Our seats were at the front, next to three long tables for the most important newspaper reporters.

Eloise said, "This place surely is crowded!"

"Aye, lass, isn't it grand?" said Mr. Scopes. "Reminds me of my days on the railroad, working a passenger train at rush hour."

I noticed the three microphones in front of the judge's bench. "You think people are listening in Chicago?" I asked Mr. Scopes.

"Afraid not," he said. "The technicians have been working on those microphones for the past hour. Said they have to send off for some parts, which won't be here until tomorrow."

"I guess the people in Chicago will have to wait," I said.

"They're not the only ones," said Mr. Scopes. "Those microphones are for the loudspeakers outside, too. The folks on the lawn aren't going to be happy."

"Well, if it isn't Monkey Girl," someone said. I whirled around and saw H. L. Mencken seated at a press table just a few feet away.

"I am not a monkey girl!" I said.

"It's a compliment," he replied. "I happen to like monkeys."

"You are so . . . rude!"

He grinned. "It's one of my best qualities."

When he turned away, Eloise whispered, "Who is he?"

I described my experience the previous day, including what Edmund Duffy had told me about H. L. Mencken. I noticed Duffy sitting next to Mencken, hunched over his sketch pad. Every so often he would glance up at me, then resume his drawing.

"May I see that?" I asked him.

"Sure," he said. He sketched in a few more lines, then handed me the pad. The girl in the drawing had a rounder face, straighter hair, and more freckles than the person I saw in the mirror each morning, but it was unmistakably

Frances Robinson. Next to her was an Eloise Purser with huge, mischievous eyes. Eloise gasped, then began to giggle.

"It's a caricature," I explained.

Ed nodded. "Do you like it?" he asked her.

"Yes," she said, "I think I do."

Seated beside us in the drawing was Mr. Scopes, with a bigger nose and a bushier mustache.

"Good heavens, is that me?" he asked.

"Yes, sir," Ed replied. "Could I get your name, please?"

"Thomas Scopes."

Ed said, "Scopes? Are you related to John T. Scopes?"

"I'm his father," said Mr. Scopes.

Mencken, who overheard them, hooted with laughter.

"What's so funny about that?" I asked.

"Then the kid driving that car yesterday must have been John Scopes himself," Mencken said. "Which means I was run over by the most famous criminal in the country!"

I said, "He's not a criminal!"

"He did break the law," said Eloise.

I whirled around to face her. "Will you stop saying that?"

"Well, it's true."

I glanced at Mencken, who had turned to speak with his friends.

"Eloise," I said in a low voice, "that man writes for people all over the country. We don't want him calling Johnny a criminal."

"Why do you always call him Johnny?" she asked.

I stared at her. "He's my friend."

"He believes in evolution. He's an atheist."

"Who told you that?" I asked.

"My brother. We talked about it last night."

I thought about all the families in Dayton who must have been discussing the trial. I wondered if they were saying the same thing.

"Johnny's an agnostic, not an atheist," I told her. "There's a big difference."

"Frances, his lawyer is Clarence Darrow."

"That's right," I said. "I met Mr. Darrow, and he's a nice man."

"Do you actually hope Darrow will win? And William Jennings Bryan will lose?"

"Of course I do. Johnny's innocent. He didn't do anything wrong."

Eloise said, "He's against the Bible."

"He's not against it," I said. "He just has doubts."

"My brother said he shouldn't be a teacher."

"Look," I said, suddenly angry, "if that's how you feel, maybe you shouldn't be sitting here. This seat belongs to Mr. Scopes."

She glared at me. "Maybe you're right. Maybe I don't want to sit here." She got up and moved off into the crowd.

I started to call after her, but just then there was a commotion at the door. Looking around, I saw Judge

Raulston enter the room with his wife and daughters. Raulston made his way through the crowd like a man campaigning for Congress, shaking hands and signing autographs at every turn. He seated his family, then hung his hat on a peg and headed for the bench.

About that time, Clarence Darrow appeared at the door. He had taken off his coat, revealing blue suspenders and a dingy white shirt that looked as if it had been slept in. Pulling a wadded-up handkerchief from his pocket, he mopped his face and adjusted his wire-rimmed glasses.

There were a few scattered boos, and I noticed that one of them came from Eloise, who had found a place next to the press tables with her brother, Crawford, and some of his friends.

Following Darrow into the courtroom were Dudley Field Malone, his dapper associate, and the other defense lawyers. Behind them, almost unnoticed, came Johnny Scopes, wearing a blue shirt and bow tie.

As they moved toward the front of the courtroom, Johnny spotted us and stopped to say hello.

"How are you feeling?" I asked him.

"To tell you the truth," he said, "I'm a little nervous."

Darrow, standing nearby, overheard Johnny and put a hand on his shoulder. "Don't worry, son. We'll show them a few tricks."

Behind us, cheering broke out and then a round of applause. Standing up to look, I saw William Jennings

Bryan enter the room, his coat in one hand and part of a sweet roll in the other. He finished off the sweet roll and waved to the crowd. Beside Bryan, basking in his reflected glory, came Sue Hicks, followed by Attorney General A. T. Stewart and the rest of the prosecution team. Mrs. Bryan, who suffered from arthritis, was pushed along behind in a wheelchair.

As Bryan approached the front of the courtroom, the applause grew louder, until it was almost deafening. The spectators rose to their feet, whistling and stomping. Bryan acknowledged the greeting, then approached Darrow and shook his hand. Immediately photographers and newsreel people clustered around them, snapping pictures and jostling for position. The place was in an uproar. I thought Judge Raulston might try to stop it, but instead he came over and joined the group, showing his best smile and posing for the cameras.

H. L. Mencken, never one to be shy, apparently decided he wanted a better view. He climbed on top of the press table and craned his neck, peering out over the crowd and furiously scribbling notes. At one point he looked down at Ed Duffy and crowed, "This isn't a trial. It's a zoo!"

He started to say more, but suddenly a strange look crossed his face. Beneath his feet the table wobbled, then collapsed with a crash.

THIRTEEN

here were screams, and people crowded in to see what had happened. The crush of bodies pushed me right up against H. L. Mencken, who lay sprawled on the flattened table, a cigar still clenched firmly between his teeth.

Ed Duffy helped Mencken to his feet. "Are you all right, sir?" he asked.

Mencken brushed himself off, then glanced over at me and flashed one of his obnoxious grins. "Quite a town you've got here, Monkey Girl. Can't even make a decent table."

He turned away, giving me a clear view of someone familiar standing just beyond the table. It was Crawford Purser, with his friends beside him and Eloise nearby. I noticed that Crawford and his friends were wearing work boots. Then again, so were most of the farmers at the courthouse that day, and there were a lot of them.

Judge Raulston came over to inspect the damage and ordered another table brought in. A few minutes later Mencken was seated again. Raulston made his way to the bench and pounded his gavel. "The court will come to order," he announced.

Mr. Scopes leaned over to me. "Here we go, lass," he said. "Get ready for the trial of the century."

The trial of the century? You wouldn't have known it that first day. I'm not sure what I expected—jugglers, fireworks, a brass band. What I got instead was something far more familiar: men in a hot room, talking. In fact, in some ways it wasn't much different from Robinson's Drugs, without the Coca-Colas.

We surely could have used them.

Being in that courtroom was like standing in front of Mama's oven when she pulled out a batch of corn bread. The heat rolled over you in waves, stealing your breath and coating your face with perspiration. And the fans didn't help at all, as much as I hated to admit it. Sometime before lunch, figuring I might as well get some use out of it, I sold mine to the lady behind me for a quarter.

The main thing the lawyers did that day was pick a jury. They had no trouble finding candidates because the lawn outside was crowded with people who wanted a front-row seat. The sheriff rounded up a bunch of them and brought them inside, where Attorney General Stewart and Clarence Darrow asked them endless questions, trying to find twelve men who hadn't already made up their minds about Johnny Scopes. As the questions went on and on, the crowd in the courtroom thinned out.

Next to me, Mr. Scopes chuckled. "Look at 'em leave," he said in a low voice. "Guess they're tired of all the hot air."

Finally, sometime around the middle of the afternoon, jury selection was completed. Of the group, nine were farmers, two were landlords, and one was a clerk. Nearly all of them said they were Christian, mostly Baptists and Methodists. One couldn't read, and three others said the only book they owned was the Bible.

Judge Raulston, satisfied, pounded his gavel and declared that court was adjourned until nine o'clock Monday morning.

I looked for Eloise and saw her leaving with Crawford and his friends. I moved to the front of the courtroom, where a group of reporters cornered Johnny Scopes and asked what he thought of it all.

"I really couldn't say," he told them. "I'm just a teacher."

As they drifted off, Johnny saw me approaching. "Let's get out of here," he said. "I can hardly breathe."

Outside we saw another cluster of reporters. In the middle, holding forth like Clarence Darrow himself, was old Mr. Scopes.

". . . I'm for Johnny," he was saying, "not only as a father but as an evolutionist myself."

Johnny groaned. "I was afraid of this. He loves to talk."

"It's kind of funny," Mr. Scopes went on, "taking a vacation to see your son go on trial as a criminal. But the lad hasn't done anything wrong. He's a chip off the old block, and I'm proud of him."

Johnny made his way through the crowd to his father. "Pop, could we talk for a minute? Privately?"

"Of course," said Mr. Scopes. "But first, say cheese!"

Johnny glanced around, and a flashbulb went off. Mr. Scopes laughed. "There'll be a divorce in the family when Mother sees this picture. Her last word when she packed my toothbrush was, 'Now, Father, don't talk to reporters and don't be photographed!'"

Johnny looked at me and sighed. As he did, the photographers closed in and the reporters began pelting him with questions.

Left by myself, I became aware of a low rumbling sound. It grew louder and more pronounced, like the approach of some strange animal herd. But the sound wasn't coming from just one direction; it seemed to surround me on all sides. It turned into a growling, bleating noise, accompanied by angry shouts.

A cloud of smoke blew past my face, and I turned around to find H. L. Mencken standing beside me, puffing on a cigar.

"Congratulations," he said, grinning. "Dayton, Tennessee, is having its first traffic jam."

I looked again and saw what he meant. With court adjourned for the weekend, all the visitors had tried to leave town at once. As a result the streets were packed with automobiles, honking and racing their engines, going absolutely nowhere.

"Welcome to the modern world," said Mencken.

Standing next to him was a small man wearing a black coat and hat. His skin was olive colored, and a curl of hair came down next to each ear.

Mencken said to me, "Didn't anybody tell you it's not polite to stare?"

I tore away my gaze, furious to realize that he was right.

"This is Rabbi Herman Rosenwasser," said Mencken. "Rabbi, this is Monkey Girl."

"My name is Frances Robinson," I snapped. I offered the man my hand, determined to show him I had some manners. He grasped it gently and shook.

"So, Frances," said Mencken, "do you know what a rabbi is? Come to think of it, have you ever met a Jew before?"

"Of course I have." I didn't tell him that the one I'd met was only part Jewish. It was old Mr. Sweeney, who owned a pig farm and attended First Baptist Church.

"Rabbi Rosenwasser came here all the way from San Francisco. He's an expert on the Bible and may be testifying next week."

I gazed at the odd little man, and it occurred to me that in the world beyond the mountains there were millions of people who were unlike anyone in Dayton. They had different languages and different beliefs. They worshipped in different ways, or not at all. There had been a time when that would have frightened me, but that day, looking at Rabbi Rosenwasser, I found myself eager to meet them.

"Rabbi," said Mencken, "how about giving her a taste of what she'll hear you say at the trial?"

Rosenwasser looked at me, his eyes twinkling. "Well, young lady," he said, "I'll simply point out that if the Bible is the inspired word of God, then one must ask, 'What language was God speaking?'"

"What do you think, Frances?" asked Mencken.

"Well," I said, "the Bible's written in English."

Mencken cackled happily. "There you go, Rabbi. You heard it."

"Creation is described in the book of Genesis," said Rosenwasser, "and Genesis was written in Hebrew. The King James Bible, the version you know, was a translation."

"Imagine that—a god who didn't speak English," said Mencken. "It's downright un-American."

"The King James Bible was written in 1611," Rosenwasser went on, "and at that time little was known of the Hebrew language. As a result your Bible contains many errors."

"Errors?" I said. "What do you mean?"

"Inaccurate translations. For instance, there's the term 'creation' itself. The Hebrew word is 'bara,' which does not exactly mean 'to create.' A better translation would be 'to set in motion.' It's a critical distinction because the correct translation seems to allow for the idea of evolution."

"In other words," said Mencken, "this whole trial may be based on a three-hundred-year-old mistake."

"Is that really true?" I asked Rosenwasser.

He smiled. "I'll leave that for the judge and jury to decide."

"Never underestimate the power of the written word," Mencken said. "For instance, look at this little gem. I bought it from a farmer before the trial." He reached into his jacket pocket and pulled out one of my father's booklets about the trial. "This is all about Dayton, the pride of the South."

"My father wrote that," I told him proudly.

"It says 'Robinson's Drugs.' Does your father own the drug store?"

"Yes, sir," I said. "You've probably seen our sign: 'Robinson's Drug Store, Where It Started.'"

"Of course," he said, nodding in recognition. "Yesterday I stumbled in there looking for whiskey. Unfortunately, I had to settle for a glass of Coca-Cola. Awful stuff. No kick at all."

"My father did a lot more than just write a book about the trial," I said. "He and his friends thought up the idea to begin with. That's what the sign means."

I told him the story, starting with the tennis game and ending with the arrest of Johnny Scopes. When I finished, Mencken threw back his head and laughed. "You mean this whole thing was a publicity stunt? To draw attention to Dayton?"

"That's right," I said. "What's so funny?"

He looked at me thoughtfully, puffing on his cigar. "You really don't understand, do you? If your father wants publicity, he's certainly getting his wish. He's made Dayton the laughingstock of the whole world."

He grinned, and suddenly I wanted to hit him. I wanted to smash his cigar and see the pain in his eyes. But I couldn't bring myself to do it because deep down inside I was afraid he might be right. It made me hate him all the more, and hate myself for thinking it.

I needed to get away—from Mencken, from the cigar smoke, from the traffic, from all the people who had overrun my town.

"Excuse me," I mumbled.

I pushed my way through the crowd and crossed the street to our house. I was headed upstairs to my room when Mama called out, "Frances, is that you?"

"Yes, ma'am." I went into the kitchen, where I found her making a batch of strawberry pies.

"Sonny's playing at Richland Creek," she said. "Would you mind going to fetch him, please?"

"Do I have to?"

Mama shot me a look.

"Can I at least have some pie?" I asked.

She cut a slice and handed it to me on a napkin. I took it and had turned to leave when she said, "How was the trial? Anything exciting happen?"

I tried to remember it, but all I could think of was Mencken's words. I shrugged. "They picked the jury. That's about all."

She smiled. "Thanks for the report." I kissed her on the cheek and headed out the door, eating as I went.

Richland Creek was a good-size stream that ran along the edge of town a few blocks east of Market Street. Sonny often went there to fish on hot summer afternoons, and sure enough that's where I found him. The surprise was that Johnny Scopes was there too.

Johnny sat under a bridge fifty yards up the creek from Sonny, skipping stones across the water. I waved to Sonny and made my way to the bridge.

"Want some company?" I asked Johnny.

"Sure, have a seat. I've been coming here in the afternoons to get away from all the people. Promise you won't tell anyone?"

"Promise," I said.

Sitting next to him on the bank, I picked up a smooth, round stone and tossed it into the creek. When it hit, a circle formed and widened. I thought of the day at Robinson's when Johnny had agreed to help Daddy and his friends, and I wondered how far the ripples would spread.

"Do you think having this trial was a mistake?" I asked.

Johnny said, "It's too late to worry about that. It's happening. That's all that matters."

"H. L. Mencken says people are laughing at Dayton."

"They aren't laughing yet, but they might," said Johnny. "It all depends."

"On what?" I asked.

"On what the reporters write. And of all the reporters, the one most people will read is H. L. Mencken."

"He's an awful man," I said.

"Then why do you keep talking to him?" asked Johnny.

"It's him, not me. He won't leave me alone."

Johnny said, "Whatever you think of him, it wasn't Mencken who started this. It was Dayton. If people end up laughing at us, we'll have no one to blame but ourselves."

"Daddy thinks it's going to be fine. He says we're getting lots of free publicity."

Johnny plucked a blade of grass and chewed on it thoughtfully. "Nothing's free, kiddo. There's always a price." He lay back on the bank and gazed at the sky. A hawk circled overhead, riding an updraft to the clouds.

"I envy that hawk," Johnny said.

"Why?"

"He can go where he wants, do as he pleases. It must be nice."

I said, "You can too."

"Not anymore," he said. "Everybody has plans for me—the Progressive Club, the ACLU, Clarence Darrow and his friends. I couldn't leave if I wanted to."

"But you're famous."

He shook his head. "They know my name. They don't know me."

"Anyway," I said, "in a few weeks you'll be able to forget this whole thing and do whatever you want."

"That's where you're wrong," he said. "As long as my name is Scopes, I won't be able to escape. You wait and see."

I didn't have to wait for long. The very next night, trying to get away from all the attention, Johnny drove up to the Morgan Springs Hotel to go to the dance, where he ran across Myrna Maxwell. They did the Charleston and a waltz or two, then Myrna asked Johnny to walk her from the dance pavilion to the hotel.

As soon as they stepped onto the path, Myrna grabbed Johnny around the neck and gave him a big kiss. I guess he figured Myrna wasn't mad at him anymore, until a moment later, when a light went on and a photographer popped out from behind a tree to take their picture.

It came out later that the whole thing had been planned. Myrna had set Johnny up, and in exchange she got her picture in papers across the country.

I asked her whose idea it was. She claimed it was hers, but I didn't believe her for a minute. The people who had planned it were smarter than Myrna. They knew that some folks thought Johnny was a womanizer, and this might raise doubts about his character. They knew that a picture was worth a thousand words.

They knew the value of publicity.

FOURTEEN

Johnny's picture in the paper wasn't the only excitement that weekend. William Jennings Bryan preached at our church on Sunday, and just about everyone who hadn't left town showed up to hear him, including Judge Raulston and his family.

Mama, Daddy, Sonny, and I were in the first row, in our usual places. I listened as Bryan went on for over an hour about the trial, which he said was a holy crusade against science and the people who wanted to destroy Christianity.

Thinking about his comments, I found myself torn. Part of me wanted to jump up and say that he was talking about Johnny Scopes, not some wild-eyed devil. Another part, hearing the kind of sermon I'd been getting my whole life, wanted nothing more than to grab the words and hold on tight, wrapping them around me like an old, familiar blanket.

On the way out I saw Eloise and her family. She said, "What are you doing here? I thought you hated William Jennings Bryan."

"I don't hate him," I said. "I'm just not as sure about things as you are. Anyway, it's my church too."

"How can you not be sure? You heard what Mr. Bryan said. Those people want to destroy Christianity."

"I've talked to Clarence Darrow, Eloise. He doesn't have horns and pointed ears. He wants to help Johnny."

She shook her head, then moved off with her brother, Crawford, and the rest of her family.

Walking home, I caught up with Daddy. "How do you feel about the trial so far?" I asked.

"They're just getting started. Ask me in a week."

"Too bad about the problems," I said.

"Problems?"

"You know. The trouble at the Mansion. The press table at the courthouse. The picture of Mr. Scopes in the paper this morning. Seems like the only one with no problems is Mr. Bryan."

He glanced at me. "What are you saying?"

"It's a little funny, that's all. People in town are rooting for Mr. Bryan, and he's not having any problems."

Daddy spotted a neighbor across the street and waved to her. "Mornin', Miss Hallahan." He lowered his voice. "Stomach trouble. Goes through more Pepto-Bismol than anyone in town."

"So," I said, "what do you think?"

"About what?"

"You know. The problems."

"I think you have an active imagination," he said.

"You hear a lot of rumors at the store. Do people think someone in town might be behind it all?"

"Sweetheart, if I listened to all the rumors, my brain would seize up and you'd have to run the store. You wouldn't want that, would you?"

"I guess not."

He put his arm around my shoulders and squeezed. "You're still my best girl, aren't you?"

"Yes, sir."

We walked a little farther. My stomach was churning. Finally I turned to him. "I need to know, Daddy. I want you to look at me and tell me the truth. I need to believe that you are strong and good and the very best man in Dayton."

He stared at me for a moment. Then he chuckled. "Of course I am, sweetheart. Of course I am."

As we got close to home, I noticed some activity on the courthouse lawn. I told Mama and Daddy I wanted to look around for a few minutes, then went over to see what was going on. As I approached, I saw H. L. Mencken puffing on a cigar. Not far away Ed Duffy was sketching on a pad.

"Hey, Monkey Girl, where've you been?" asked Mencken.

"At church. Mr. Bryan gave the sermon. I'm surprised you weren't there."

He laughed. "I'll be hearing enough of Bryan's

sermons at the courthouse. Besides, tonight I'm going to hear the real thing—Brother Joe Furdew."

"You mean the Holy Roller?" I asked.

"That's right," said Mencken. "I'm tired of this whining, simpering, watered-down Christianity. I want some meat and potatoes."

I had heard people talk about Brother Joe Furdew and the revival meetings he'd been holding outside of town, but the thought of actually going to hear him had never occurred to me. For one thing, most folks said Furdew was crazy. Besides, I knew Mama and Daddy would never have allowed me to go. They said his version of the Bible was more like a Hollywood movie, and his Holy Roller followers were "common." That meant low-class, and it was about the worst thing Daddy ever said about anybody.

"You don't really believe what he preaches, do you?" I asked Mencken.

He laughed. "Of course not, but I understand he puts on a whale of a show. Want to go with us?"

"Me? No, I couldn't."

"What's wrong?" he said. "Are you scared?"

"Of course not!"

He eyed me thoughtfully. "I think you are. You've convinced yourself that the people rooting for Bryan are nice, normal folks. But they're not, you know. Most of them are Bible-thumping lunatics, and you're scared to death you might be one of them."

"That's ridiculous," I said.

"Then go with us," he said. "Come on, Monkey Girl, I dare you." He crossed his arms and leaned back, grinning through a thick cloud of cigar smoke.

Something about his expression made me furious. "No," I exclaimed, "and that's final!"

He shrugged. "Have it your way. Come on, Duffy, let's get going."

Ed put away his sketch pad, and the two of them headed for their car, a black Ford parked around the side of the courthouse. As I watched them go, I thought about Mencken. Why did he make me so angry? Part of it was his smirk and his know-it-all manner. But it was more than that. Mencken disagreed with just about everything my father said. That meant that on almost any topic, including Brother Joe Furdew, if Mencken was right then Daddy must be wrong.

I was still thinking about it that night as Mama and I finished washing the dishes after supper. "Can I go visit Eloise Purser?" I asked her.

"*May* I go visit Eloise Purser," she said.

"Please, may I? I want to talk to her about something."

Mama put away the last of the silverware. "Yes, you may. You've been good about helping your father at the store, and I know he appreciates it." She gave me a peck on the cheek. "Now, get going before I think of something else for you to do."

As I hurried outside, I heard Sonny squawk, "Hey, how come she gets to go out and I don't?" I didn't wait to hear the answer.

It was still light outside, and plenty hot. I skipped across our front lawn, which was starting to turn brown in the summer sun, and headed for Eloise Purser's house. When I got there I kept right on going.

I went up Market to Sixth Street, where Dr. A. M. Morgan lived. I had heard that Dr. Morgan and his wife had gone to the mountains during the trial and rented their house to H. L. Mencken and his friends. Sure enough, the black Ford was parked at the curb next to a row of hedges.

Glancing around, I darted between the car and the hedges. Satisfied no one had seen me, I tried the handle on the Ford's back door. It was unlocked. I opened it as quietly as I could and looked inside. The backseat was filled with boxes, blankets, and other things. There wasn't room to sit, but there was enough space on the floor to lie down if you were small enough. I squeezed in, pulled a blanket over me, and waited.

Soon I realized I'd made a bad mistake. The car must have been sitting in the sun for several hours, because it was hot as a furnace. Within minutes I was drenched with sweat. The blanket wasn't helping any, so I took it off and peered out the window. I couldn't see much because of the hedges, but it didn't appear that anyone was coming, so I rolled down the window on each side, hoping to get a draft going.

Just then I heard voices.

I pulled the blanket back over my head and sat as still as I could. As the voices came closer, I recognized one of them as H. L. Mencken's.

"... and I told him, 'Well, if you're the Bible champion, I'd love to see the guy who came in second place.'"

There was laughter, and Ed Duffy said, "Didn't we leave the windows closed?"

"Search me," Mencken replied. "You're the driver."

A third voice said, "Who cares? There's nothing in the car worth taking."

"I guess you're right," Ed said.

I heard the front doors open. "I'll ride shotgun," said Mencken. "Kent, you get in back."

There was a click, and the door next to me opened. I held my breath, trying desperately to figure out what I would do when they found me.

"Good Lord, it's a pigsty," Kent said. "Mencken, is all of this yours?"

"Just a few odds and ends. Push it over and get in."

"Odds and ends?" said Kent. "There's a couple of typewriters back here."

"You can never have too many typewriters," Mencken said.

"And here's a New Jersey phone book. Where'd you get this stuff?"

Mencken said, "Is my unabridged dictionary back there? I couldn't find it in the house."

"It's possible," said Kent. "It's possible the French Foreign Legion is here too." The door closed. "I'm sitting in front. Move over."

I breathed a sigh of relief and shifted slightly, trying to find a comfortable position. Meanwhile the engine started and the car began to move.

Kent said, "Traveling with you is like spending time with my Aunt Stella."

"Does she smoke cigars?" Mencken asked.

"She collects things and constantly complains about her health."

"I don't complain unless it's serious," said Mencken.

Kent said, "Do you really believe you had the bubonic plague?"

"I'm telling you, I had the symptoms."

"And strep throat and malaria, all at the same time?"

"Slow down!" Mencken screamed. "There's a car coming!"

Ed patiently explained, "It's a block away, and I'm only going twelve miles an hour."

"That's another thing," Kent said. "Why don't you drive once in a while?"

"Then I wouldn't be able to yell at Duffy," said Mencken.

Before long the sun had set, and the light grew dim enough so I could safely peek out from beneath the blanket. We were on a winding, bumpy route that jarred my bones and made me feel like I was going to throw up, a condition that wasn't helped by Mencken's cigar smoke.

Suddenly Mencken called out, "There! See that light in the trees? That's their signal!"

I risked a glance out the window and saw a point of light winking at us from the woods.

"Why don't they just get a building and put up a sign?" asked Kent.

"It's not a church; it's a revival meeting," said Mencken. "Besides, a church wouldn't be big enough."

Ed said, "You really think there are people out there? We're a million miles from nowhere."

"Just wait," Mencken said. "You'll see."

Rounding a curve, we found a pasture filled with horses, horse-drawn wagons, and a few cars. Ed parked at the edge of the pasture, and the three of them piled out. I waited until they were a safe distance away, then got out and followed.

FIFTEEN

I followed Mencken and his friends across the pasture and through the woods, and soon I made out the sound of someone shouting.

". . . and I'm-a telling you, the Lord will cast down the high kings into the dirt—Glory to God!—he certainly will—Glory to God!—for Jesus was a humble feller—Glory to God!—and when the great day comes—Glory to God!—what can any of 'em do but jump up and say—Glory to God!—I ain't nothin', Lord, I ain't nothin'—Glory to God!—Glory to God!—Glory to God!"

Up ahead, in a clearing half the size of a football field, three lanterns had been set on the ground. Next to the lanterns strode Brother Joe Furdew, a thin, hatchet-faced man in blue jeans, bellowing to the skies. Three giant shadows strode along with him, jumping up and down, waving their arms, dancing in the light of the lanterns. At the foot of the shadows, on rows of wooden benches, sat hundreds of the people known as Holy Rollers. There were farmers, mountain men, children, and rough country women in homemade dresses.

"Glory to God!" they shouted back, rocking to and fro in the moonlight.

Brother Furdew fell silent, and a small woman leaped to her feet. She told how a book salesman had come to her house and she had sent him away, refusing even to touch the books.

"Why read books at all?" she declared. "If what's in a book is true, then it's already in the Bible. If it's not true, then I'm risking my soul to read it. Better to burn the books. Glory to God!"

Behind her a man in dirty overalls stood up. "Education is the devil's work!" he cried. "Cities are his unholy breeding ground. Dayton is Sodom, and Morgantown ain't much better. I say, send 'em all to hell!"

There were shouts of agreement, and someone called for a hymn. A chubby man wearing wire-rimmed glasses stepped forward and led the group in singing. At the end of the hymn, instead of stopping, the crowd began a low chant. A group of men moved one of the benches to the front of the clearing, and a young woman threw herself onto it, wailing.

"This sister has asked for prayers," said Brother Furdew.

The chanting grew louder, and people moved to the front, surrounding the young woman, all of them shouting out prayers. Brother Furdew knelt next to her, placed his bony hand on her head, and began his own prayer, strong and urgent, almost angry. He asked God to forgive the woman, to beat back the demons that possessed her and bring her to the light.

Suddenly Furdew jumped to his feet and began babbling and gurgling, the way Daddy sometimes did when he brushed his teeth. The people joined in, making strange animal noises—mewing like sheep, howling like dogs, screeching like cats in the night. Some of them bounced and skittered around the bench, arching their backs, then doubling over like they had a bellyache.

I must have edged out from behind the trees to get a better look, because when Mencken glanced around he spotted me. A look of surprise crossed his face, and he motioned for me to join him. Sheepishly I made my way forward.

"So, you decided to come after all," he said.

Ed Duffy asked, "How did you get here?"

Sue Hicks always said honesty is the best policy, especially if you've been caught. I stammered, "I—I came with you. I was in the backseat. I'm sorry."

Ed gazed at me in shock. "Well, I'll be."

Mencken said, "You know you're going to hell, don't you?" Then he grinned. "And I'll be right there beside you."

"You're not mad?" I asked.

He puffed his cigar and said, "Not at all. It shows gumption."

"Really?"

"Sure. Now all you have to do is learn how to lie, cheat, and steal, and you can be a reporter."

Nearby, the man called Kent was taking notes as he watched the service. Mencken said, "Hey, Kent, you want to get closer?"

"Think we can?"

"Just follow me," said Mencken, stepping out from behind the trees.

Kent glanced nervously at the worshippers. "You're sure they won't mind?"

Mencken laughed. "They won't even notice."

With that, he marched all the way to the front row and sat down. Kent did the same, and Ed joined them, sketching furiously. I settled in beside them. Sure enough, the few people left in their seats were too absorbed in the service to look at us.

By that time there were so many worshippers crowded around the young woman that we could barely see her, even though she was no more than ten feet away. They would jump around for a while, then throw themselves back into the group, eventually forming a writhing pile three or four deep. Every so often one of the worshippers would bounce off and come stumbling into us, then turn and go back for more.

We saw every kind of person you could imagine. A large, sweaty woman in a gingham dress slumped to the ground, praying. An elderly man in patched overalls crawled by, inspecting the ground. Next to us, a young mother shouted out Bible quotations, feeding her baby at the same time. One man, smoking a cigar, hopped around the worshippers doing something that looked a lot like the Charleston. When he turned and waved to me, I realized it was Mencken.

"You should try this," he called.

Kent hissed, "Get away from there!"

Mencken just laughed. He danced for a while longer, then came back and plopped down on the bench.

Kent said, "It won't be so funny if they find out we're reporters."

"Aw, don't be such a killjoy," said Mencken. "The only thing dangerous about this group is their smell."

Kent closed his notebook. "I say we get out of here. Are you finished, Duffy?"

I leaned over to see what Ed was doing. It was a drawing of the worshippers heaped on top of each other, with arms and legs sticking out of the pile along with the occasional Bible.

What struck me most vividly were the faces. They were twisted, distorted, barely human. I wanted to turn away but couldn't. All I could think was that if you scratched the surface, is that what my town was like? Is that what my father was like? Is that what I was like?

Could it be that Mencken was right? In spite of the heat, I found myself shivering.

Ed sketched another line or two, then closed the tablet. "Done," he said.

We retraced our steps through the woods and returned to the car, where I got in back, wedging myself in next to a stack of typing paper.

"Well, Monkey Girl, what did you think?" asked Mencken as we bumped along the country road toward town.

For once I didn't say anything about the name. I guess I was too busy pondering what I had seen.

"I never knew there were people like that," I told him.

Mencken said, "They're not so different from you Baptists."

"I'm a Methodist."

"That's even worse," he said.

"We don't yell and jump around like that."

Mencken said, "Ah, yes, but secretly you want to. Holy Rollers are just Methodists without inhibitions."

"That's not true!"

"It's all based on emotion," he said. "At least these people admit it. After all, if you're going with feelings over logic, why not go all the way? Burn the books! Close down the schools! It feels right, so do it."

"You're twisting everything around."

"What you were looking at back there—that's what the trial's all about. Take away the judicial robes and the manners and the fancy words, and it's just a bunch of Holy Rollers thrashing around in the woods. It's funny and it's sad and it stinks to high heaven. And it has nothing whatever to do with justice."

SIXTEEN

It was nine thirty when they dropped me off, but the courthouse lawn was still crowded with people. Crossing the street to my house, I hurried up the porch steps and was headed for the front door when I heard a voice in the darkness.

"Hello, Frances."

It was Daddy. He sat motionless on the porch swing.

"Frances," he said, "I'd like you to come sit beside me, please, ma'am."

Something in me shrank. There was a cold, formal quality to his voice that usually meant trouble.

I crossed the porch and sat down next to him. Nothing moved—not Daddy or the swing or the thick, heavy air.

"Your mother called Mrs. Purser to see how you were doing," said Daddy. "It seems you weren't there."

I said softly, "No, sir, I wasn't."

"And why not?"

"I was . . . doing something else," I said.

"Are you going to tell me what it was?" he asked.

I took a deep breath. "Well, sir, it's like this. I went to see the Holy Rollers."

"You *what*?" He stared at me as if I'd told him I had just returned from Mars.

I said, "You know—the people who hold revival meetings outside of town?"

"I know who they are," said Daddy. "What I don't know is why in God's name my daughter would be interested."

"I was curious. I wanted to see what they were like."

"How did you get there?" asked Daddy. "It's out past Morgantown, isn't it?"

I started to tell him, then remembered Daddy's opinion of reporters, which was somewhere between a skunk and a bank robber.

"There were people offering rides from the courthouse," I said. "I went on a truck with some other folks."

"Good Lord, do you know what those people do? They jump and twitch like wild animals."

"Yes, sir, you might say that."

He said, "They're crazy. They must be."

"They believe in Jesus," I said.

"Jesus? Sweetheart, trust me, the Jesus those people worship is nobody you'd recognize."

Agitated, he got up from the swing and paced back and forth, then turned to face me. "Frances," he said, "what you did was foolish and dangerous, but that's not what upsets me the most. The worst thing is that you lied. You looked your mama straight in the eye and you lied." He stared at me, hard. "Well? Isn't that right?"

"Yes, sir."

"And if we hadn't found out from Mrs. Purser, you would have kept right on lying."

"Daddy—"

"It's true and you know it," he said. "Frances, in our family lying is unacceptable. It is completely and totally unacceptable. Do you hear me?"

"Yes, sir."

"To make sure you understand the seriousness of what you've done, I'm confining you to the house for a week."

I looked back at him, stunned. "You mean, I can't go outside at all?"

"You can help me at the store. And go to church."

"What about the trial?" I asked. "In a week it might be over."

"I can't help that."

"Daddy, that's not fair. You said yourself, this trial's the biggest thing that ever hit Dayton. I don't want to miss it. I can't."

"Then maybe you'll think twice before you lie again."

They were deciding the fate of Johnny Scopes, the man I loved, and I wasn't going to be there? I couldn't believe it, couldn't accept it.

I said, "I made a mistake. I know that. But I don't deserve this."

"In this family we tell the truth and we keep our word," he said. "Why do you think people come to Robinson's?"

I thought of the sign at Daddy's store: ROBINSON'S DRUG STORE, WHERE IT STARTED. Then I thought of Johnny at the creek, tossing pebbles into the water and saying his life would never be the same. And I knew what I had to say.

"I did wrong," I said, my voice quivering, "but maybe I'm not the only one."

"Sweetheart, don't try to pass the blame."

"I'm talking about you," I said.

"Me?"

"You asked Mr. Scopes to help Dayton and promised him nothing bad would happen," I said. "But it did."

"Like what?"

I said, "Everybody wants something from him. He can't go any place without people pestering him, like Myrna Maxwell giving him that kiss."

"I doubt he's too upset about that," said Daddy, flashing me a smile.

It occurred to me that with Daddy a smile didn't always mean he was happy. He also did it when things got tense, as a way of calming people down. There was a particular smile he used when he was in a tight spot. I'd seen him do it a hundred times at the store when customers were upset. It was a tool of the trade, like his prescription pad or the cash register. Now he was using it on me, and I didn't like it. I felt something rising up inside me, and suddenly it burst out.

"Don't talk to me about lying," I said, "because that's all you've been doing for the past two months."

Daddy's smile disappeared, and his eyes narrowed. The expression on his face told me to stop, but I couldn't.

"You're always talking about publicity," I said. "What else is it but lies? Dayton isn't some garden spot. It's a little town with problems. People are moving away, and the ones who stay are stubborn and small-minded. They're set in their ways. They won't listen to new ideas.

"You told Johnny Scopes not to worry because you'd take care of everything. Now look at him. He's miserable. He hates the trial. All he wants to do is go back to his teaching job, but you won't give him a contract."

"Who told you that?" Daddy demanded.

"I was there when you talked to him, remember?"

He waved away my question with a flick of his hand. "That's school business. It doesn't concern you."

"We keep our word, Daddy. That's what you said. Maybe I told a lie, but so did you."

His eyes were narrow, and his face wore an expression I'd never seen before. "There are some things you don't understand," he said.

"Daddy, I'm fifteen years old. I *do* understand, and I want to know more. I want to know all kinds of things.

What's evolution? What's an agnostic? Who are the Holy Rollers? That's why I went tonight. I wanted to know, and I knew you wouldn't like it."

"You're right about that," he snapped.

"Don't make me miss the trial," I said. "I need to see what happens. I need to understand. Please?"

He stared at me for a long time, then took a deep breath and peered off into the night. "I'm tired," he said. "So are you. I think it's time for bed."

"What about the trial?"

"Don't push me, Frances."

"I need to know."

"This conversation is over," he said.

I studied his face. Then I moved past him and went inside. I could feel his gaze hot against my back as I climbed the stairs, went into my room, and shut the door.

SEVENTEEN

When I woke up on Monday morning, Mama was sitting on the edge of my bed. "I talked to your father last night," she said. "He told me what you did."

I looked up groggily. "Which part?"

"The Holy Rollers. I already knew about the lie." It was just a word, but coming from Mama's lips it jolted me, like a slap across the face.

She said, "This is serious, you know. Your father was right to punish you."

"But Mama—"

She held up her hand. "I agree with the punishment, but I'm not so sure about the timing. The trial's important. I'd hate for you to miss it. I told your father that."

"Maybe I should go talk to him."

"Maybe. But don't press him. It needs to be his idea. And whatever you do, don't tell him we spoke."

I leaned over and kissed her. "Thank you, Mama."

She went downstairs to make breakfast. I put on my

robe and went to look for Daddy. I found him in the bathroom, shaving.

Lowering the toilet lid, I sat down and watched him. Daddy shaved the way he cleaned his store, slowly and methodically, making sure everything was just right. The steady scratching of his razor seemed to echo off the walls.

"I've been thinking," he said. "Maybe I was a little harsh last night. It was wrong, what you did, especially the lie. I want you to understand that."

"Yes, sir, I do."

"But it's also important for you to see the trial. It's a historical event. I'm still confining you to the house, but the punishment won't start until the trial's over. You can go see it, as long as I don't need you at the store."

I jumped up and hugged him around the waist. "Thank you, Daddy!"

"Just one more thing," he said. "Seems to me I wasn't the only one who was a little harsh last night."

"I was upset," I said, my heart pounding.

"It's one thing to be upset. It's another thing to question someone's word."

Part of me wanted to throw myself into his arms. But another part was thinking of Johnny, remembering the anger and determination on his face. I wondered how it would feel to be in his arms.

"Daddy, I'd like to say it's all right, but it's not. Mr.

Scopes is doing just what you asked him to do. I think you should give him his contract."

Daddy studied me for a moment, his gaze turning hard and flat. "I see." He lifted his razor once again. "Would you excuse me, Frances? I need to finish shaving."

I stood there for a moment, hoping he would look back at me. He never did.

When I went down to breakfast a few minutes later, I found Daddy standing by Mama at the stove, reading to her from the *Chattanooga Times.*

"'. . . Try a meal in the hotel; it is tasteless and swims in grease. Go to the drug store and call for refreshment: the boy will hand you almost automatically a beaker of Coca-Cola.' Well, at least he got that part right."

I reached for a glass of orange juice. "What are you reading, Daddy?"

"A newspaper report about Dayton. Written by a fellow named Mencken, from Baltimore."

My hand slipped, spilling juice across the counter.

"For heaven's sake, Frances, watch what you're doing," said Mama. She handed me a dish towel, and I blotted up the juice.

"If he's from Baltimore, why is the article in the *Chattanooga Times?*" I asked.

"The *Times* is reprinting the articles," said Daddy. "Unfortunately, so are a lot of other papers across the country. It seems Mr. Mencken has a following."

"Is the article bad?" I asked.

"It's fine if you don't mind being called a yokel or a primate."

Sonny said, "What's a primate?" He was crouched on his chair with strawberry jam smeared across his mouth and chin, which for some reason made Mama chuckle.

"It's another name for monkey," she told him. "Not that we have any in this house."

"It's no laughing matter," Daddy said. "People are going to read this and think we're a bunch of fools and hicks. Why doesn't he mention our friendly people or well-run businesses?"

"Those things don't sell newspapers," said Mama. "You know that, dear."

Daddy went back to the table, shaking his head in disgust. I got some eggs and bacon and sat down next to him. As soon as he put down the paper, I picked it up and read the article.

"Some of this really makes me mad," I said when I finished reading. "But he's right about one thing. No jury in Dayton would give Mr. Scopes a fair trial."

Daddy said, "What are you talking about?"

"They're against evolution. They've already made up their minds."

Daddy gave me a funny look. "'They'?"

"You know—the people in Dayton."

"You live in Dayton," he said. "You're against evolution. Aren't you?"

I said, "You saw the jury. It's a bunch of Baptists and Methodists. Some of them said the only book they read is the Bible."

"You didn't answer my question," said Daddy.

Mama said, "More biscuits, anyone?"

"Yes, ma'am!" said Sonny.

Daddy looked at me. "Frances, do you believe in evolution?"

"Mr. Scopes does."

"Forget John Scopes."

"No!" I said. "He's the nicest person in this town. He's starting to hate it here, and I can't blame him. You know, the world doesn't begin and end in Dayton. There are lots of people out there. They don't believe the same things we do. I met one of them Friday. He was a rabbi. He looked different from us, but you know what? He was a nice man. He reads the Bible too, and he says it doesn't say anything against evolution."

"That's absurd," said Daddy.

"I'd sooner agree with him than with those Holy Rollers," I said.

"I told you, they're crazy," he said.

"What's a Holy Roller?" asked Sonny.

Mama said, "Nothing you need to worry about."

Daddy took one last sip of coffee and rose from the table. "I need to get to the store. Frances, are you coming? Or would you rather explore the world?"

"You go ahead," I said. "I'll be there as soon as I finish my breakfast."

I finished a few minutes later and headed for the store. On the way I passed the courthouse. Even though it was early, the temperature was in the nineties and the lawn was already crowded with people.

"Frances!" someone called. I looked around and saw Crawford Purser.

"I heard you and Eloise are having a fight," he said.

"It's not a fight. It's just . . . a disagreement."

He said, "Do you really believe in evolution?"

"I wish people would stop asking me that! I don't know what I think. But at least I'm thinking, which is more than I can say for most people in this town."

He gave me a funny look. "Are you all right?"

"I'm fine!"

Crawford looked around. "It sure is a big crowd. I saw a man with a newsreel camera. He said Dayton's going to be famous."

"That's not necessarily good."

I told him about H. L. Mencken's article that made fun of Dayton and that had been printed in newspapers around the country. As I finished, I heard a familiar laugh and saw Mencken chatting with Reverend T. T. Martin on the courthouse lawn.

"There he is now," I said. "That's H. L. Mencken."

"The one with the cigar?" asked Crawford.

I nodded. "That's him. See you later."

I approached Mencken, who spotted me and grinned. "Well, if it's not Monkey Girl."

"Now, Henry," said T. T. Martin, "we're not going to get into that again, are we?"

"Aw, she doesn't mind. She's a real sport. You should have seen her last night, hopping around the woods with Brother Joe Furdew."

"I did no such thing," I said. "Anyway, that's not why I'm here. Mr. Mencken, I need to talk to you."

"See that?" he said to Martin. "The way she squints her eyes when she's upset? Definitely apelike. No question."

"I saw your article in the paper this morning," I said.

"Ah, yes, the *Chattanooga Times*," he said. "I was surprised. Didn't know they had such good taste."

"You're making Dayton look bad."

"I can't take credit for that," he said. "You people did all the work."

"Will you please stop making wisecracks and just listen?" I said.

His eyebrows shot up, and he looked at me thoughtfully, puffing on his cigar. "Go on," he said.

"We're not primates, and we're not yokels. There are plenty of smart people in Dayton, and nice ones too. You're hurting them all when you write those things."

"Hallelujah!" said T. T. Martin. "She's a natural-born preacher!"

Mencken gazed at me. "Is that all?"

"No, it's not," I said. "I've eaten at the Aqua Hotel, and their food is delicious."

Mencken started to laugh, then caught himself. "Sorry, I thought you were joking."

"Well, Henry," said T. T. Martin, "what do you have to say for yourself? Those are some pretty serious charges."

"I'd say I'm the least of her worries," said Mencken.

"What's that supposed to mean?" I asked.

"It's like with me and my friend T. T. here. I think he's crazy, but I tell him to his face, just like I do with Dayton. I'm honest, and I say exactly how I feel. You're a bunch of Bible-thumping extremists, and you couldn't put on a fair trial if your lives depended on it. But that doesn't mean I don't like you."

"Is that supposed to make me feel good?" I asked.

"At least you know where I stand," he said. "Not like those other people."

"What people?"

"Some of the other reporters. They're nice to your face, then they turn around and criticize you behind your back. For instance, one fellow's not even going to the trial. He already knows what his editor wants him to write, and, believe me, it's nothing you'd like. So he just hangs around his hotel room playing cards. Pleasant young fellow. He'll tip his hat to you if he sees you on the street. Just don't turn your back on him."

There was a thump. Mencken grunted, then stumbled and nearly fell. He whirled and scanned the area.

"What's wrong?" asked Martin.

Leaning over, Mencken picked up a rock the size of a golf ball. "Somebody threw this and hit me in the back," he said.

I looked around, wondering who could have done it. There were lots of people, and none of them seemed to be looking in our direction. Suddenly, I saw a flash of color behind some trees and spotted three boys running away. For a second I couldn't make out who they were, then one of them turned and looked back at us. It was a boy from school named Zeke Cunningham. I had only spoken to him once or twice, but I did know one thing. He was a friend of Crawford Purser.

EIGHTEEN

It was a big day at the store. The crowds had come back to town after the weekend, and a lot of them stopped at Robinson's for a cold drink before going to the courthouse. I worked at the cash register and behind the soda fountain, and at lunch Mama and I waited on tables. Business finally slowed down that afternoon, and I asked Daddy if I could go to the trial.

"What did I tell you this morning?" he said.

"You told me I could go if you didn't need me at the store."

"Then go," he said, turning away.

I had thought maybe he would be mad, but this was almost worse. It was as if he didn't care.

Mama put her arm around me. "Pay close attention to the trial," she said. "Remember, you're not listening just for yourself—it's for your children and grandchildren, too."

I imagined myself with children all around, telling stories about the trial. Sitting next to me was my husband, a tall, handsome man with blond hair. It was Johnny Scopes.

As I approached the courthouse, I heard the voice of Judge Raulston booming out from loudspeakers on the lawn. Apparently the men from Chicago had fixed their microphones over the weekend, which meant that people far beyond the boundaries of Dayton were listening as well.

I slipped inside the courtroom and looked for old Mr. Scopes. He was saving a seat, just like before.

"What did I miss?" I asked, slipping in beside him.

"As far as the trial's concerned, not much," he said in a low voice. "But there was some excitement. See that woman over there?" He pointed to a tall lady with bright red hair and colorful clothes, who was sitting near the front. "People are calling her the mystery woman. She paraded in this morning like the Queen of Sheba, ordering people around and talking in a loud voice. Somebody said she's the niece of General Gordon, a Confederate general, but no one's quite sure."

As I looked at the woman, she noticed that I was watching and turned to stare at me. She had green eyes, and lipstick that looked as if it had been put on with a trowel. The woman held my gaze for a moment, then lifted her nose and turned away.

The heat in the courtroom was stifling, but Dudley Field Malone still wore a vest, a starched collar, and a perfectly pressed suit. Malone was standing before the jury, making the claim that Tennessee law favored the Bible and promoted Christianity over other religions, which was unconstitutional.

"What I mean is this," said Malone. "If there be a single child or young man or young woman in your school who is a Jew, to impose a particular view of creation from the Bible is interfering, from our point of view, with his civil rights under our theory of the case. That is our contention."

When Malone finished, Clarence Darrow rose to his feet. Unlike his friend, Darrow had taken off his jacket, revealing a wrinkled shirt and a pair of orange suspenders. The crowd chattered excitedly, eager to hear the world-famous lawyer.

Darrow turned to the judge. "Here we find today as brazen and bold an attempt to destroy learning as was ever made in the Middle Ages. The only difference is, we have not provided that the defendant shall be burned at the stake. But there is a time for that, Your Honor. We have to approach things gradually."

Darrow began pacing back and forth in front of the jury, his voice rising and falling as he spoke. He maintained that the evolution law violated the United States Constitution, especially the amendment providing for the separation of church and state.

"The state of Tennessee," he said, "has no more right to teach the Bible as the divine book than that the Koran is one, or the Book of Mormon, or the book of Confucius, of the Buddha, of the essays of Emerson, or any one of the ten thousand books to which human souls have gone for consolation and aid in their troubles."

I had never heard of some of those books and was surprised that Darrow mentioned them alongside the Bible. I wondered what it would be like to read them.

Darrow went on talking about the Bible. He said he didn't pretend to be an expert, but he did know a few basic things.

"The Bible is not one book," he said. "The Bible is made up of sixty-six books written over a period of about one thousand years. It is a book primarily of religion and morals. It is not a book of science—never was and never was meant to be. In it there is nothing described that would tell you how to build a railroad or a steamboat. It is not a book on geology; its authors knew nothing about geology. It is not a book on biology; they knew nothing about it. And yet the lawmakers of Tennessee have made the Bible the yardstick to measure every man's learning.

"Are your mathematics good? Turn to First Elijah two. Is your philosophy good? See Second Samuel three. Is your astronomy good? See Genesis, chapter two, verse seven. Is your chemistry good? See Deuteronomy three, six, or anything that tells about brimstone. Every bit of knowledge that the mind has must be submitted to a religious test."

I pictured my chemistry class at school and some of the experiments we did with our teacher, Mr. Carruthers. I wondered what Jesus would do with a Bunsen burner.

Darrow's voice grew louder and his gestures bolder. He flung his arms about and in so doing managed to tear his sleeve. The tear got bigger and bigger, fluttering like a flag as he spoke.

"If today you can take a thing like evolution and make it a crime to teach it in the public school, tomorrow you can make it a crime to teach it in the private school or the church. At the next session you may ban books and the newspapers. Soon you may set Catholic against Protestant and Protestant against Protestant, and try to foist your own religion upon the minds of men.

"After a while, Your Honor, it is the setting of man against man and creed against creed, until with flying banners and beating drums we are marching backward to the glorious ages of the sixteenth century, when bigots lighted fires to burn the men who dared to bring any intelligence and enlightenment and culture to the human mind."

NINETEEN

When Darrow finished, Judge Raulston adjourned the court with a whack of his gavel, and the place broke out in excited chatter. From what people were saying, they were in agreement on one thing: Clarence Darrow might be an agent of the devil, but he surely knew how to give a speech.

At the press table a few feet away, H. L. Mencken watched the jury and shook his head.

"Look at them," he said to Ed Duffy. "Darrow gave them plenty to talk about, and they're still sitting there like tree stumps. He might as well have shouted up a rain spout for all the good it did."

I looked for Johnny Scopes but didn't see him. I threaded my way through the crowd and down the stairway and finally reached the front door. Scanning the courthouse lawn, I caught sight of Johnny walking down Market Street, jacket over his arm and hat tipped back on his head. I hurried after him.

By the time I crossed Market, Johnny had turned east

on First Street. I started to call to him, then noticed someone with gaudy clothes and bright red hair twenty yards ahead of me. It was the mystery woman.

She was with a man I didn't recognize, and the two of them were moving purposefully, their eyes glued to Johnny. When he stopped, they stopped. He glanced over his shoulder once, and they immediately halted and looked in a store window, pretending to shop.

Johnny veered off First Street and headed for the bridge over Richland Creek, where I had found him Friday. The mystery woman and her friend followed, and I trailed behind, curious to see what they would do. Johnny disappeared down the creek bank. I moved quickly to a tree at the top of the bank where I could see what would happen.

Johnny climbed onto a big, flat rock, set down his coat and hat, and took off his shirt. Lying down on the rock, he stretched out in the sun and closed his eyes. The mystery woman circled around and began sneaking up behind him. When she stepped onto the rock, I yelled, "Johnny, look out!"

He opened his eyes just in time to see the woman kneel down and slip her arm around him. Her friend appeared from behind a tree, pulled out a camera, and snapped a picture. It would show Johnny, shirtless, lounging with the mystery woman.

"Let's go!" said the photographer.

As the woman got up to leave, Johnny scrambled to his feet and tried to grab her. She gave him a shove. He teetered for a moment on the edge of the rock, then fell backward into the creek with a splash. The woman, meanwhile, jumped to dry ground and ran off toward town with her friend.

I sprinted down the bank, arriving at the creek a moment later. Johnny was lying on his back in a shallow pool, his body half-submerged.

"Are you all right?" I asked. I offered my hand, but he just stared up at the sky. All of a sudden he started to laugh. It came from somewhere deep inside, and it went on and on. I found myself smiling, and finally I laughed too, out of sheer relief that he was fine. At last he stopped and just lay there in the water, grinning.

"Aren't you going to get up?" I asked.

He said, "Why? This is the coolest I've been in weeks."

"Do you want me to go look for that woman?"

His smile faded, replaced by a thoughtful expression that seemed almost bitter. Propping himself up on his elbows, he looked around. "It's too late. She's gone."

"Who were they?" I asked.

He said, "I don't know about her, but I recognized him. He was the same man who took my picture with Myrna. I have a feeling I'm going to be in the paper again."

"Why is he doing it?"

He shook his head in disgust. "For money or

headlines or maybe just sheer malice. Who knows?"

He lay there for a moment longer, then climbed to his feet, his clothes soaked. "Don't ever grow up, Frances," he said.

"What do you mean?"

"When you're young, you think everybody's honest and good and wants the best for you," he said. "It's not like that. Most people want something from you—your help, your privacy, your good name. And they don't give anything in return."

"Are you talking about the trial?" I asked.

"What else is there?"

He put his shirt back on, settled onto the rock, and leaned back to enjoy the sunshine. Sitting down next to him, I said, "It's not going to look good. First Myrna, now this."

"Yeah," he said. "Good old Myrna."

"I hate her."

"In a way she's not so different from this whole town," he said. "They grab you, give you a kiss, and about the time you start to enjoy it, you find out it was all a setup. They just wanted their picture in the paper."

Johnny was too nice to say it, but I knew he was talking about my father and his plans to get publicity for Dayton. "It's not fair, what they're doing to you," I said.

"What's that got to do with it?" He gestured toward the creek. "The minnows eat the insects. The trout eat the minnows. We eat the trout. That's how the world works.

It's got nothing to do with fairness. Ask Mr. Darwin—he'll tell you."

"Sounds pretty grim to me," I said.

"Sometimes I think so too."

Talking about Darwin reminded me of the trial. "What did you think of Mr. Darrow's speech?" I asked.

"It was all right," he said.

"You didn't like it?"

"It was great. He just made it sound as if the fate of the world were resting on my shoulders. I mean, my God, if I lose this case, people are going to start burning each other at the stake again."

"Still," I said, "I think you're lucky to have him."

"I heard Darrow talking to the other lawyers before the trial today," said Johnny. "They're cooking up something. I don't know exactly what, but it has to do with Bryan. They say they're going to destroy him."

"You know how lawyers exaggerate," I said. "Sue Hicks does it all the time."

"I'm not so sure," said Johnny. "This trial does something to people. It makes them crazy and mean."

I thought of H. L. Mencken. I thought of my father. "Why?" I said. "Why does it have to be like that?"

"I wish I knew. Something about getting people's attention. Something about wanting a thing so badly you'll do anything to get it."

Johnny gazed up at the sky. "I'm tired of it," he said. "I'm tired, period."

I thought of all the things he had done for our town—befriending students, coaching the football team, even teaching science class. We certainly were choosing an odd way to thank him.

I looked down at him. He seemed older than before. There were lines on his forehead that I had never noticed. He had always smiled a lot, but today his mouth was turned down at the corners, the way his father's mouth was. When he spoke, his voice had a rough, gravelly sound, not at all like the voice that had called out plays when I watched football practice. The sparkle was gone from his eyes.

I wondered what those eyes saw when they looked at me. Maybe a little sister. Maybe more. He was only nine years older than I was. It might seem like a lot now, but when I was twenty he'd be twenty-nine. When I was thirty he'd be thirty-nine. It wasn't really such a big difference.

My mother told me once that love changes over time, like fire. It starts off blazing, and then, as the years pass, the flames die back. They burn gently, steadily, with enough heat and light to last a lifetime.

It seemed like years since I'd gone to play tennis with Johnny. That day, I'd thought he was young and handsome and perfect in every way. He was older now, and so was I. He wasn't perfect. He wasn't sure of what he was doing.

He wasn't sure of what he believed. All he knew was that he had agreed to help the town, and he was going to keep his word.

I wasn't sure of what I was doing either. Things were all mixed up. So was I. But I knew one thing. I loved Johnny Scopes. It had seemed exciting and romantic that day on the tennis court. Now it seemed calmer, steadier, like something I could live with for a long time.

"Is there anything I can do to help?" I asked.

"Keep being my friend."

I studied the curve of his cheek and wondered what it would be like to kiss him. I felt my cheeks grow red at the thought and quickly pushed it away.

"Frances!" someone called from down the creek.

It was Sonny, carrying a fishing pole and bucket. I quickly jumped to my feet, worried that he might guess what I had been thinking.

Sonny approached and said, "Hi, Mr. Scopes."

Johnny smiled. "Hello there, Sonny. Hey, did you know that your sister just rescued me from the creek?"

Sonny's eyes opened wide. "Really?"

Johnny told him what had happened, then said, "She's a good friend, and a sweet kid on top of it."

I grimaced. His words made me feel like a cute, harmless dog.

Sonny picked up his bucket. "I guess I'll get going. I've got some fishing to do."

After he had left, Johnny turned to me. "Frances, I really meant that about being a friend. You know how many friends I have—I mean, really good friends? People I can sit down with like this and just talk? Only a few. Maybe two or three in this whole town."

He plucked a blade of grass and chewed on it thoughtfully. "Friends have your best interests at heart. They stand by you when times are tough. They tell you the truth, even if you don't want to hear it."

I thought of Eloise. "What if two friends have an argument? What if they stop talking to each other?"

"It depends," he said. "Are they really, truly friends?"

"Yes."

"Well, then, it might take a while, but they'll find a way to start talking again."

Johnny sat up on the rock and stretched. "I'd better be going," he said. "I have a meeting with the lawyers tonight at the Mansion."

He walked me back to town. When I got home, I went to the kitchen looking for something to eat. As I got some of Mama's peach cobbler from the icebox, I heard a sound behind me and glanced back to see Daddy standing in the doorway.

"Think I could have some of that?" he asked.

"All right," I said. I spooned some onto a couple of plates and took them to the table, where we set about eating it. Neither of us spoke for a while.

Finally Daddy said, "How was the trial?"

"It was good. I'm glad I went."

"Did you see any history being made?"

"Maybe a little." I told him about Darrow's speech, and how he had compared the trial to something out of the Middle Ages, when they burned people at the stake. "He thinks people in Dayton are a bunch of religious fanatics," I said.

Daddy grunted. "Don't listen to that man. He's an atheist."

"I wish people would stop saying that. He's an agnostic."

It wasn't often that I contradicted my father. I wondered if he would get mad.

His expression didn't change, but his face grew flushed. "Let me tell you something," he said with feeling. "Dayton's just a little town, no doubt about it. We don't have all that big-city hoorah, like fancy restaurants and theaters and ladies wearing genuine mink coats. But as I look around me, I see good people. Honest people. People who tell you the truth, even if it isn't pretty. Those people believe that the Bible is the revealed wisdom of God and every word in it is true. Now, does that make them religious fanatics? Maybe so. But if I blow out a tire on Highway 27 and need some help, who would be more likely to stop? A religious fanatic in a Model T, or some big-city agnostic in a limousine?"

He wanted me to answer, but somehow I felt as if that would be giving in. I just sat there, and so did he. Finally he took his plate to the sink, rinsed it off, and left the room.

I said good night to Mama, then climbed the stairs to my room and got ready for bed. Before going to sleep I went over to the window.

I looked up and saw the moon moving behind the clouds. Or maybe the clouds were moving and the moon was standing still. Then I realized that everything was moving—the moon, the clouds, the earth, my town. The very house I sat in was whirling through space, speeding, shifting, changing as it went. And so was I.

PART THREE

THE TRUTH

That the rising town of Dayton, when it put the infidel Scopes on trial, bit off far more than it has been able to chew—this melancholy fact must now be evident to everyone. The village Aristides Sophocles Goldsboroughs believed that the trial would bring in a lot of money, and produce a vast mass of free and profitable advertising. They were wrong on both counts, as boomers usually are. Very little money was actually spent by the visitors: the adjacent yokels brought their own lunches and went home to sleep, and the city men from afar rushed down to Chattanooga whenever there was a lull. As for the advertising that went out over the leased wires, I greatly fear that it has quite ruined the town. When people recall it hereafter they will think of it as they think of Herrin, Ill., and Homestead, Pa. It will be a joke town at best, and infamous at worst.

—H. L. Mencken
The Baltimore Evening Sun
July 20, 1925

TWENTY

You could always tell when things slowed down at the trial, because business picked up at Robinson's. On Tuesday the store was crowded with customers, and, sure enough, they reported that the lawyers were arguing about minor details. I had been hoping to go to the trial again but, hearing the reports, decided to stay at the store and help out. As it turned out, that's where all the action was.

News, gossip, and rumors were flying all day. It got worse when the afternoon papers came in, showing Johnny's photo with the mystery woman. I tried to explain what had happened, but people didn't want to hear it.

As if that weren't bad enough, somebody started a rumor about one of Johnny's lawyers. The first I heard of it was when Billy Langford came by the counter and said, "Hey, did you hear? Some lady's checking into the hotel to stay with Dudley Field Malone, and it's not his wife."

A reporter threw some change on the counter, grabbed his jacket and notepad, and headed for the door. I looked around for Daddy but didn't see him, so I took off my apron and handed it to Sonny.

"I'm going next door. Tell Daddy I'll be back in a few minutes."

Before Sonny could say anything I was out the door, following the reporter down the sidewalk. We ducked into the Aqua Hotel, where the lobby was filled with people.

I pushed my way through the crowd, and at the front, standing by the check-in desk, was a tall, dark-haired woman with the glamorous looks of a movie star. She was wearing a diamond necklace and enough rings for half the women in Dayton. But it wasn't her face or the jewelry, beautiful as they were, that caught my eye; it was her clothes. She was one of the few women I had ever seen who wore pants.

There was the flash of a camera, and I saw the photographer who had followed Johnny the day before. Next to him was a reporter with a pad and pencil.

"Miss Stevens," he asked, "is it true that you'll be staying with Dudley Field Malone?"

"Yes, it is," she said.

"And how does his wife feel about that?" said the reporter, smirking.

Miss Stevens flashed a dazzling smile. "Dudley's wife and I have an understanding."

An excited buzz broke out. The reporter's eyebrows flew upward, and he began furiously taking notes. My heart sank.

Whoever had tipped off the reporters must be smiling now.

Finally someone shouted, "What's the understanding?"

"Why don't you ask his wife?" said Miss Stevens. "She's here in the room."

The reporters craned their necks, looking for Mrs. Malone. The only person they saw who might fit the role was Rowena Butcher, a widow who spent most of her time at the Aqua looking for eligible men. When a reporter asked Rowena if she was married to Dudley Field Malone, she said, "No, but I'd be happy to talk to him."

Miss Stevens laughed and said, "You boys don't get it, do you? Well, I certainly hope you know more about the trial than you know about me. My name is Doris Stevens, and if you had done a little research you would have learned that *I'm* Dudley's wife. I also happen to be a feminist. In case you don't know what that is, it means I believe in equal rights for women."

"So you're Mrs. Malone?" asked one of the reporters.

"No, I'm not," she said. When the reporter looked puzzled, she smiled sweetly and said, "Let me ask you something. When you got married, did you take your wife's last name?"

"Of course not," he said.

"Then why should I? I'm proud of my family and want to keep my own last name. So please address me as Miss Stevens."

"Where did you get those pants?" someone asked.

"Do you like them?" she replied. "You can try them on if you'd like."

There were whoops of laughter, and the reporter's face turned red. The man next to him said, "Miss Stevens, what do you think of the Scopes trial?"

"Why should I care?" she said. "It's strictly for men. The plaintiff is a man. The judge is a man. The lawyers are men. The witnesses are men. All the people on the jury are men. And think about this: Everyone is so concerned about Mr. Scopes teaching evolution to his students, but it's only the boys they talk about. No one ever mentions the girls. What about them? They have just as much right to be corrupted, don't they?"

Another reporter asked, "Did you ever think about becoming a lawyer? You'd fit right in."

She grinned. "I don't know whether that's a compliment or an insult."

The bellman arrived with her bags, and she said, "Sorry, boys, but it was a long, hot trip, and I'm ready for a bath. See you around town."

As she followed the bellman up the stairs, a flashbulb went off, and I spotted the photographer again. Hurrying over, I tugged on his sleeve. He glanced down at me, annoyed.

"Yeah, what is it?" he said.

"I saw you at the creek yesterday," I said, "sneaking around with that mystery woman. Why are you doing this, anyway?"

"Girlie, it's how I make my living."

"You're hurting people. Did you ever think about that?" He turned away, but I grabbed his sleeve again. My heart pounding, I said, "Who asked you to do it?"

"What are you talking about?"

"Someone is giving you these tips," I said. "I want to know who."

He looked down, as if seeing me for the first time. "Who are you, anyway?"

"I'm Frances Robinson. My father owns the drug store."

He laughed. "The drug store? Now isn't that a coincidence."

"What's that supposed to mean?"

"Believe me, you don't want to know." He turned to leave.

"Tell me!" I said. He shook his head and walked out the door.

I looked around the room and noticed a familiar face. It was Crawford Purser. I caught up with him and said, "You seem to be pretty interested in the trial."

He said, "So is everybody else in town."

"What did you think of her?" I asked.

"That woman? She's beautiful. Kind of strange, though."

I said, "Do you think she's right? Is the trial really just for men?"

He shrugged. "So's the whole world. Nothing new about that."

"My mother might disagree," I said.

"She can disagree all she wants. They still wouldn't let her on the jury."

"It's not right," I said.

He gave me a funny look. "So, are you one of those feminists she was talking about?"

"No!"

"Are you an agnostic?" he asked.

"Did Eloise tell you that?"

"She says you're rooting for Clarence Darrow."

"I'm a friend of Johnny Scopes," I said. "I thought you were too."

He said, "I don't have a problem with Mr. Scopes. It's Clarence Darrow and his friends who bother me."

"That's what somebody else thought. They tried to sabotage the Mansion. I don't suppose you know anything about that."

"No, I don't," he said.

"What about H. L. Mencken? Did you throw rocks at him yesterday?"

"Who's H. L. Mencken?" he said.

"The newspaperman. The one with the cigar. Remember, I pointed him out to you?"

He looked away. "There's a lot of reporters around town. I can't remember all of them."

"I saw Zeke Cunningham do it. He's a friend of yours."

Crawford looked back at me, angry. "I can't keep track of what Zeke Cunningham does. If you want to know about it, go talk to him." He glanced at the big clock in front of the jewelry store. "It's getting late. I have some chores to do. I'll see you later."

He turned and hurried off. As I watched him go, I wondered why he had gotten so angry. And something else occurred to me. He had never answered my question.

TWENTY-ONE

Wednesday was Daddy's day to testify at the trial. Mama offered to watch the store while he was gone, but Daddy would have none of it.

"Nonsense!" he said. "The whole family's going to the trial."

"Even me?" asked Sonny.

"Darn tootin'!"

Sonny jumped up and down. "Oh, boy! I'm going to see the monkeys!"

Daddy arranged for Billy Langford to watch the store, and we headed for the courthouse.

A. T. Stewart, one of the prosecution lawyers, was presenting the case against Johnny. He called Walter White, superintendent of schools, to establish what had happened that day at Robinson's. The next witnesses were two of Johnny's students. As Doris Stevens had pointed out, both of them were boys: Howard Morgan and Bud Shelton.

Bud described what Johnny had taught the class about evolution. When he finished, Clarence Darrow rose to cross-examine him. Darrow, wearing another wrinkled shirt, gave Bud a friendly smile.

"How old are you?" asked Darrow.

"Seventeen."

"Professor Scopes said that all forms of life came from a single cell, didn't he?"

"Yes, sir," Bud said.

Darrow hooked his thumbs behind a pair of bright red suspenders. "Are you a church member?" he asked.

"Yes, sir."

"Do you still belong?"

Bud said, "Yes, sir."

"You didn't leave church when he told you all forms of life began with a single cell?"

"No, sir."

"That is all," said Darrow.

Bud returned to his seat, and the bailiff looked at his list of witnesses. "The court calls F. E. Robinson," he announced.

Daddy made his way to the front, where he took his place on the witness stand. He didn't look nervous, like Howard or Bud; in fact, I could see that he was enjoying himself. I could almost hear him composing the story he'd be telling customers for years, about the time he testified at the famous Scopes trial.

Stewart approached him and said, "You are Robinson, of Robinson's Drug Store?"

"Yes, sir."

"Where all this started?"

"Yes, sir," Daddy said proudly.

Stewart took Daddy through his version of the meeting at Robinson's, then nodded to Darrow. "You may cross-examine."

Darrow picked up a copy of the *Civic Biology* textbook and showed it to Daddy. "You were selling these, were you not?"

"Yes, sir."

"While at the same time you were a member of the school board?" asked Darrow.

"Yes, sir."

Darrow chuckled. "I think someone ought to advise you that you are not bound to answer these questions."

Some people in the courtroom laughed. Daddy grinned.

"What's so funny?" I asked Mama.

"Mr. Darrow seems to think it's a conflict of interest," Mama said. "That's when you use a position of authority to make money for yourself."

"Did Daddy do that?" I asked.

"Hush," said Mama. "Let's listen."

Darrow said, "How many of those did you have for sale?"

"Oh, I've been selling that book for six or seven years," Daddy replied.

"Have you noticed any mental or moral deterioration growing out of the thing?" asked Darrow.

Stewart objected, and Judge Raulston agreed, instructing Darrow to withdraw the question. Darrow did so, then asked Daddy what part of the book Johnny had taught from. Daddy read the section on evolution.

As he read, I found myself getting angry. Daddy had sold the book and made money doing it, while Johnny had taught from the book and might go to jail. It didn't seem right.

When Daddy finished reading, Darrow thanked him, and he was excused. Daddy came back to his seat, chatting and shaking hands with people the whole way.

The prosecution rested, which meant it was time for the defense to present its case in favor of Johnny. The first witness was Professor Maynard M. Metcalf, one of a long list of scientists Darrow was hoping to parade before the court to talk about evolution. Metcalf, a short, plump, balding man who wore glasses, was a professor of zoology at Johns Hopkins University and taught a Bible study class at his church on Sundays.

Darrow took him through a long series of questions about his background, then asked, "Would you say that most scientific men in the world are evolutionists?"

Stewart leaped from his chair to object, saying that Metcalf couldn't speak for all the scientists in the world. Finally they settled on a compromise: Metcalf would be allowed to enter his testimony into the record, and then the next day both sides would argue the question of whether that testimony was admissible.

Darrow, Stewart, Judge Raulston, and the court reporter gathered around Metcalf and heard his answer in private, so it could be entered into the record. Metcalf wasn't very good at whispering, so I was able to hear what he said.

"I am acquainted with practically all of the zoologists, botonists, and geologists of this country who have done important work," said Metcalf, "and I am absolutely convinced that all these men believe that evolution is a fact."

When Professor Metcalf finished, Judge Raulston went back to his chair and pounded the gavel.

"Court dismissed until nine o'clock tomorrow," he said.

TWENTY-TWO

That afternoon just about everyone in town came by the store to slap Daddy on the back and talk about his big day in court. I watched for a while without saying anything, but finally I couldn't stand it anymore.

I waited for business to slow down a little bit, then pulled Daddy aside.

"Why do you seem so happy?" I asked.

"I'm famous, darlin'. Your daddy testified at the Scopes trial."

"Aren't you embarrassed?"

"About what?" he asked.

"Mr. Scopes is on trial for teaching that textbook," I said, "and you're the one who sold it to him."

He shrugged. "I own a store. I sell lots of things."

"This one might send a man to jail."

"Frances, he's not going to jail. I told you that."

"What about his reputation?" I asked. "You know what people are saying? He's an atheist. He's an outsider. He's not fit to teach our children."

"It'll blow over," he said.

"Then why don't you send him a contract? He wants to teach, and you don't even care." My father had hurt Johnny, and I wanted to hurt him back. "You've been grinning and shaking hands. You think everything is fine. Well, you know what? Some people don't think so. They say your publicity scheme has backfired, and Dayton's the laughingstock of the world."

Daddy's eyes flashed. "Who have you been talking to?"

"Wake up, Daddy. Look around. Listen. People are making fun of Dayton. They're calling it Monkey Town."

He stared at me, his mouth set in a tight, hard line.

Just then the front door swung open, and Billy Langford pushed his way through, loaded down with newspapers.

"Mr. Earle, the Chattanooga papers came in," he called.

Daddy gazed at me for another moment, then twisted his face into a grin and turned away. "Excellent!" he replied. "Set 'em down over here, son."

Billy lugged the papers to the counter, followed by a line of people who wanted to buy them. Daddy took one of the papers and began reading it. He frowned.

"What's wrong?" asked Billy.

"It's that Mencken fellow again. He came down hard on Mr. Bryan, and on Dayton, too."

Daddy read, "'Bryan understands these peasants, and they understand him. . . . The fellow is full of such bitter, implacable hatreds that they radiate from him like heat from a stove.'"

A group of customers had gathered around. Hearing this, they started to grumble. Daddy went on.

"'He hates the learning that he cannot grasp. He hates those who sneer at him. He hates, in general, all who stand apart from his own pathetic commonness. And the yokels hate with him, some of them almost as bitterly as he does himself. They are willing and eager to follow him—and he has already given them a taste of blood.'"

A woman standing nearby looked around at the other customers, her eyes flashing. "'Peasants'! 'Yokels'! Who is this Mencken fellow, anyway?"

Daddy didn't say a word. He just closed the newspaper, folded it up, and stuffed it in the trash.

The customers cheered. As the noise died down, a short, squat figure pushed his way through the crowd.

It was H. L. Mencken.

Daddy, who didn't recognize him, watched as Mencken lifted the paper from the trash and smoothed the pages.

"I'll take this if you don't need it," said Mencken. He took the cigar from his mouth and extended his hand. "H. L. Mencken's the name. My friends call me Henry. My enemies call me worse."

A fierce rumble broke out among the customers. Daddy stared at the extended hand but did nothing, so Mencken dropped it. Glancing over at me, he started to say hello, then decided not to. I can't say I was sorry.

Daddy said, "Mr. Mencken, that's the most hateful, damaging, one-sided piece of journalism I've ever read."

"Thank you," said Mencken, grinning.

Someone at the back of the crowd called out, "You won't be smiling if you keep it up."

A man next to me spoke up. I recognized him as Mr. Carter, a farmer who had a place outside of town. "What do you have against the South?" he demanded.

"It's great if you're a mosquito," said Mencken.

Mr. Carter took a step forward. Daddy restrained him and said, "As you can tell, Mr. Mencken, we're pretty upset. You're ruining the reputation of our town."

Mencken shrugged. "I'm a journalist. I just write what I see."

Daddy said, "I know something about journalism, and you, sir, are not a journalist. You're a parasite."

Mencken gazed at him coolly. He took a puff of his cigar and blew a cloud of smoke toward the ceiling.

"Dayton's a fine place," he said. "It looks even better after a jug of moonshine, as my colleagues and I discovered last night. Which brings me to the reason for my visit. Do you have anything for a hangover?"

Someone yelled out, "How about arsenic?" No one laughed.

Daddy eyed Mencken for a long time. "I recommend Coca-Cola," he said.

"I thought that was just a fountain drink," said Mencken.

"No," Daddy said, "it helps headaches and indigestion, plus it's a good pick-me-up."

"Is that what you tell your customers?" asked Mencken.

"Every day of the world," said Daddy.

Mencken scratched his chin. "Now, isn't that interesting. I could swear that the Coca-Cola Company admitted their drink has no medicinal properties whatsoever."

Somebody said, "That's crazy! You tell him, Mr. Earle."

Daddy stood there, his eyes locked onto Mencken's. Neither of them moved. The store grew quiet as everyone waited to see what would happen.

Finally Daddy said, "I still recommend it to my customers. But what you say is true."

The store was deathly still. Daddy turned away and began straightening the shelves behind him.

Mr. Carter growled, "Go home, Mencken. We don't want you around here."

The people edged forward. Mencken eyed them and said under his breath, "I love Dayton." Then he made his way through the crowd and was gone.

I was looking out my window that night before bed, when there was a knock at the door and Daddy peered inside.

"Can I come in?" he asked.

"I guess so."

He came in and stood beside me. Even though the window was open, there wasn't the barest hint of a breeze. He pulled a handkerchief from his pocket and wiped off his forehead.

"You'd think it would cool off when the sun went down," he said. "Worst heat I can remember."

I didn't answer. He said, "You and I are having our troubles these days, aren't we?"

"I used to believe everything you told me. Now I wonder about all of it. Even Coca-Cola."

"Pardon me?" he said.

"What you've been telling people about Coca-Cola— it's a lie, isn't it?"

"Not exactly."

"It wasn't the truth."

He said, "We could go outside right now and find a hundred people who would swear Coca-Cola made them feel better."

"That doesn't mean it was right," I said.

"I taught you well, didn't I?"

"Yes, sir, you did." I looked up at him. The moonlight made his face look pale. "Daddy, why did you do it?"

He folded and refolded the handkerchief. Then he wiped off his forehead again. "I'm a salesman. That's what I do. I sell things."

"Like textbooks?"

"Like anything. Pills, bandages, screwdrivers, kites, newspapers, kitchen utensils. And, yes, textbooks."

I said, "Even if they're used against someone?"

"Look, Frances, I know you're upset," he said. "I didn't come in here to make excuses or explain things away. I want to tell you the truth, as near as I can. The truth is, I'm just a person like you who's doing his best to get by. Sometimes I make mistakes. Sometimes I stretch the truth. Sometimes I push too hard to make a sale.

"I know Coca-Cola's not a medicine. But people want to believe it, so I go along with them. I know that textbooks can be misused, but my customers want to buy them, so I oblige. I won't defend it, except to say I was earning money for you and Sonny and Mama. My intentions were perfect, even if I'm not."

"What about evolution?" I asked.

"What about it?"

"Mr. Scopes believes it. Clarence Darrow believes it. That professor said all the scientists believe it. Maybe you're wrong about that, too."

"That's different," he said.

"Why?"

"I stretch the truth once in a while, but God doesn't. Read your Bible. It's right there in black and white."

"You really think all those scientists are wrong?" I asked.

"Don't take my word for it," said Daddy. "Mr. Bryan's talking tomorrow. You can go hear him."

"I heard him already at church. Besides, I think he's strange. He says he's on a diet but won't stop eating."

"William Jennings Bryan is a great man. He was almost president."

I said, "I think he's a salesman too. He's selling the Bible."

"Frances!"

"It's true, isn't it?"

Daddy said, "If Mr. Bryan is a salesman, then so is Clarence Darrow. I'll take the Bible over evolution any day."

"Where does that leave Mr. Scopes?"

"What about him?"

I said, "Everyone's so busy selling, they've forgotten who's on trial. They don't even look at him. It's like he's not there."

"This trial isn't about John Scopes," said Daddy. "It's about the truth."

"I thought it was about publicity," I said.

He stared at me hard, then looked out the window. The hills in the distance were black, like something cut out of construction paper and glued across the sky.

"Never saw such heat," he said.

"I wish none of this ever happened," I said. "I wish we could go back to the way we were."

"You and me? Or the town?"

"Everybody. All of us. We're out of control. We're changing into something different."

"Is it really so bad?" he asked.

I said, "Dayton was going to be famous. Mr. Scopes was going to be fine."

"He will be. Just be patient." He wiped his forehead again.

"Daddy?" I said.

He turned to look at me, his body outlined against the window frame. There had been a time when he would have filled it, but now he seemed small and slight, his shoulders hunched.

"Some strange things have been happening around town," I said. "The break-in at the Mansion, photographers making Mr. Scopes look bad, reporters tipped off about Mr. Malone's wife. You don't know anything about it, do you?"

He was quiet for the longest time. Then he said, "No, I don't."

I watched him closely. He stood perfectly still. He didn't blink. He didn't twitch. Nothing moved. Not a muscle.

"I heard something at the store today," I said. "After Mr. Mencken left, there was a rumor some people were going to hurt him."

An odd look crossed his face. Was it surprise? Disgust? Recognition? I couldn't tell.

"Mencken is a miserable person," he said.

"But we aren't," I said. "Are we?"

"No. No, of course not." He put his hand on my shoulder, then slipped out the door.

TWENTY-THREE

The next day, word spread that William Jennings Bryan would speak at the trial, and the crowds swelled. Luckily, Mr. Scopes saved a seat for me, so I didn't have trouble getting in. I watched as Bryan took a drink of ice water and then rose to speak. He wore a white shirt, a bow tie, and black pants with suspenders. Like everyone else, he was sweating, and I noticed that he carried one of the fans from Robinson's Drug Store. As he approached the judge's desk, the big crowd grew quiet.

"The Christian believes man came from above," Bryan declared, "but the evolutionist believes he must have come from below—that is, from a lower order of animals."

Bryan picked up a copy of *Civic Biology* and opened it. "Your Honor, we are told just how many species there are: 518,900. Eight thousand protozoa, thirty-five hundred sponges, three hundred and sixty thousand insects."

Even reading from a textbook, Bryan's voice commanded attention. He recited the numbers, his voice rising and falling like a church organ.

"Then we have the reptiles, thirty-five hundred, and then thirteen thousand birds. And then we have mammals, thirty-five hundred, and there is a little circle and man is in the circle. Find him! Find man!

"How dare those scientists put man in a little ring like that, with lions and tigers and everything that is bad!" cried Bryan. "They cannot find a single species that came from another, and yet they demand that we allow them to teach this stuff to our children."

He stretched out his arms, and his voice filled the room. "My friends, I want you to know that they not only have no proof, but they cannot find the beginning. Not one of them can tell you how life began. They do not deal with the problems of life. They do not teach the great science of how to live. They do not talk about God."

When Bryan finished, the crowd applauded enthusiastically, going on for over a minute. Old Mr. Scopes leaned over to me.

"He's the one they came to hear, lass. If they were voting, Johnny would be in jail right now."

As they continued to applaud, Judge Raulston called on Dudley Field Malone. I wondered what Malone could possibly do to get the crowd's attention. I didn't have to wait long to find out.

Malone, who was the only lawyer on either side never to be seen wearing anything but a coat and tie, finally gave in to the heat and removed his jacket with a flourish.

"By jove." Mr. Scopes chuckled. "He's human after all!"

The crowd, shifting their attention from Bryan to Malone, actually laughed and applauded. I wondered what they would do when Malone began tearing down Bryan. To my surprise, he didn't. Instead he praised Bryan, saying that the trial was not a conflict of personalities but of ideas. For that reason, he said, it was vitally important that the long list of scientists be allowed to testify in defense of John Scopes.

Malone gestured toward the prosecution table, where Bryan rested, fanning himself. "These gentlemen say, 'The Bible contains the truth.' And we say, 'Keep your Bible. Keep it as your consolation, keep it as your guide. But keep it where it belongs, in the world of your own conscience. Do not try to tell an intelligent world that these books, written by men who knew none of the accepted fundamental facts of science, can be put into a course of science."

If Bryan's voice was an organ, Malone's was a brass band. As he built his case, the trumpets sounded, and the trombones blared.

"The truth always wins," he said, "and we are not afraid of it. The truth is no coward. The truth does not need the law. The truth does not need the forces of government. The truth does not need Mr. Bryan. The truth is imperishable, eternal, and immortal and needs no human agency to support it."

Malone strode toward Bryan and stood before him, hands on hips. "We are not afraid!" he thundered. "Where is the fear? We meet it. Where is the fear? We defy it. We ask your honor to admit the scientific evidence as a matter of correct law, as a matter of sound procedure, and as a matter of justice to the defense of this case."

Malone dropped his arms to his sides and lowered his head, like a man who had just run a mile. To my amazement, the spectators roared their approval. They leaped to their feet and clapped and hooted and cheered.

Who would have expected it? The biggest round of applause hadn't been for William Jennings Bryan or Clarence Darrow, but for the smart-talking, fancy-dressing Yankee who spoke in favor of evolution. The crowd didn't agree with him, but they just kept cheering and cheering.

When Malone returned to the defense table, the other lawyers shook his hand and pounded him on the back. Darrow leaned toward him and shouted over the crowd, "Tennessee needs only fifteen minutes of free speech to become civilized!"

H. L. Mencken, at the press table nearby, called out, "Dudley, that was absolutely and without any possible exception the loudest thing I ever heard!"

Beside me Mr. Scopes grinned. "Maybe Johnny has a chance after all," he said.

I looked at Judge Raulston, at the jurors, at the people who crowded in around me. Maybe Daddy was right—if I was in trouble, they would be more likely to help me than H. L. Mencken and his friends. But would they help Johnny Scopes? Would they listen to Malone and find Johnny innocent? Was it possible that the people of Dayton could change?

TWENTY-FOUR

Daddy came home for supper that night and then returned to the store, as he often did. I went to the parlor to practice the piano. Mama and Sonny stayed in the kitchen to bake some cookies.

I'd been practicing for thirty minutes or so when I heard a tapping noise at the window. I glanced up, and there on the lawn was Eloise Purser. She appeared to be breathing hard, and there was a desperate look in her eyes.

Eloise motioned me outside. I gestured for her to come in, but she shook her head. Getting up, I slipped through the door and onto the porch.

As I approached Eloise, I realized I was still mad at her. "Did you ever think of knocking on the door?" I snapped.

"I was afraid your parents might answer," said Eloise. "I didn't want them to know."

"About what?"

"It's about my brother. He might be in trouble. If your parents find out, they might tell mine."

"Why did you come to me?" I asked.

She looked at me, surprised. "Who else would I come to?"

I remembered what Johnny Scopes had said at the creek. Eloise and I might disagree about some things, but we were still friends.

"Your brother threw rocks at H. L. Mencken," I said.

"No, he didn't. He told me what happened. Zeke Cunningham and his friends wanted to do something bad to Mencken—you know, teach him a lesson, maybe even hurt him. Zeke got the idea of throwing rocks. Crawford didn't want to do it and told them so. They made fun of him, and he got embarrassed. He knew where Mencken was because you had shown him. So he told Zeke. Crawford didn't throw any rocks."

It made sense. Crawford got into trouble every once in a while, but he didn't seem like the kind of person who would deliberately hurt someone. Zeke Cunningham, on the other hand, was mean and everybody knew it.

Eloise said, "He felt bad about it. Maybe that's why he told me the other thing."

"What other thing?"

"Come with me and I'll show you. Please? It's an emergency."

"Maybe I should get my mother," I said.

"No! Crawford made me promise." Fidgeting, Eloise looked back over her shoulder. "I'm going. You can either come with me or not."

I studied her face and made my decision. "I'll be right back," I said.

I hurried to the kitchen, where Mama was rolling out cookie dough. Sonny stood on a stool next to her.

"Could I go out for a while?" I said.

She looked up, showing a spot of flour on her nose. "What about your practicing?"

"I'm finished. I'll do more tomorrow night."

"Why don't you help Sonny and me with these cookies?" she asked.

"I can't," I said, thinking quickly. "I promised Eloise I'd go over to her house."

"The last time you told me that, you ended up five miles out of town, watching the Holy Rollers."

"Not this time, Mama. This time it's true."

"And this time you'll stay there?"

I hesitated, but only for a moment. "Yes, ma'am."

"All right, then," said Mama. "Just don't stay out too late."

I walked calmly out of the kitchen, then streaked across the parlor and through the front door. Eloise motioned to me, and the two of us raced down Market Street.

As we ran, I thought about what I had just done. It was only a few days since I'd told Mama I would never lie to her again, and already I had broken my promise. The funny thing was, it didn't seem so bad, because I was trying to help somebody. But it still was a lie, wasn't it? Maybe it was a little bit like what Daddy had done when he told his customers that Coca-Cola was a medicine. Or maybe not.

I had always figured that the older you got, the more you'd understand. So far it wasn't turning out that way.

There was a flash of lightning, and thunderclouds moved across the sky.

"Where are we going?" I asked.

"Dayton Hardware," said Eloise, breathing hard. "There's some men planning something bad." She glanced over at me with a strange look on her face. "My brother's there."

We turned down First Street and ducked into an alley, coming up behind Dayton Hardware. Eloise gestured for me to be quiet, and we sneaked up to a window at the back of the building. She climbed on a box and looked through the window, then motioned for me to join her. I climbed up and peered inside.

A group of men had crowded into the stockroom and were seated on rough benches. In the front row was Crawford Purser. Zeke Cunningham sat nearby, whittling with a hunting knife. At the front of the room was the farmer I'd seen at the store, Mr. Carter. He paced back and forth, reading from a newspaper.

"'This old buzzard, having failed to raise the mob against its rulers, now prepares to raise it against its teachers,'" Mr. Carter read. I didn't have to see the article to know it had been written by H. L. Mencken, and the "old buzzard" was William Jennings Bryan.

"'One somehow pities him, despite his so palpable imbecilities,'" Mr. Carter went on. "'It is a tragedy, indeed, to begin life as a hero and to end it as a buffoon. But let no one, laughing at him, underestimate the magic that lies in his black, malignant eye, his frayed but still eloquent voice. He can shake and inflame these poor ignoramuses as no other man among us can shake and inflame them, and he is desperately eager to order the charge.'"

Mr. Carter looked up from the paper. "You heard it, boys. Mr. Bryan's a buffoon and we're ignoramuses."

"I'm tired of it," said one of the men, a mill worker with broad shoulders and big hands.

"I say we stop him," said another. "That's why we came here tonight, isn't it?"

Mr. Carter looked out over the group. "So, what do you say? Should we go have a talk with Mr. H. L. Mencken?"

"Maybe we can persuade him to leave town," said the mill worker. He closed his hand, making a fist the size of an anvil.

The man next to him said, "Let's give him a ride. I know where we can get some tar and feathers."

Zeke Cunningham looked up from his whittling. "Why should he leave town at all?" He reached into a canvas bag and pulled out a rope.

The room fell silent. I looked at Crawford Purser. His face was white as a sheet.

The mill worker said, "We need a plan." He looked toward the back of the room and gestured. "You planned everything else. Come up here and help us figure this out."

My view of the room was blocked on one side, so I couldn't see who he was talking to. But I had an idea. The thought of it made my body ache and my blood run cold. I hugged myself, shivering. I remembered that my father wasn't home. I recalled the look on his face when I asked about the strange things going on in town. I knew that when people in Dayton needed a plan, they usually went to F. E. Robinson.

The crowd parted, and a man made his way to the front of the room, his face in shadow. When he reached the front, he stepped into the light.

It was Billy Langford.

He looked different without a white apron. His clothes were rough, and I couldn't help but notice that he wore work boots. Suddenly things clicked into place. Billy had been off work the day I saw footprints at the Mansion. It was Billy who had told me about Doris Stevens checking into the hotel. And it was Billy who constantly had followed my father around the store, hanging on every word, learning the gospel of publicity.

"Well," Mr. Carter asked him, "got any ideas?"

Billy fidgeted, glancing over at Zeke. "Now, I don't like Mencken any more than the rest of you. But a rope . . ."

"What's wrong?" said Zeke. "Afraid to finish what you started?"

There were murmurs of agreement. Outside, the wind had started to blow. I tried to adjust my footing, and suddenly the box gave way, sending Eloise and me crashing into a stack of metal pipes. When I looked up, I saw the flash of a knife and found myself staring into the grim face of Zeke Cunningham.

"Please don't hurt us," said Eloise in a shaky voice.

Zeke looked back and forth between us. Scowling, he put away his knife and yanked us to our feet, then dragged us inside.

Crawford Purser jumped to his feet. "Eloise, what are you doing here?"

"Snooping," said Zeke. "I found them outside the window."

Mr. Carter grabbed Eloise's arm. Her eyes grew big, and she struggled to get loose.

"Let go of her," said Crawford.

"You were spying on us," said Mr. Carter, his voice low and menacing.

"So what?" I said quickly, hoping to distract Mr. Carter. "So what if we were spying on you?"

He stopped and looked at me. For a second I thought he was going to grab me, too.

"You think it's bad to spy on people?" I said. "What about beating someone up, or running him out of town?"

"How much did they hear?" asked the mill worker.

"What about tar and feathers?" I said. "I wonder what the Bible says about that."

"Shut up," said Zeke.

I looked him in the eye. My heart was racing. "What were you planning to do with that rope?" I asked.

Nobody said a word.

Zeke picked up the canvas bag. Staring straight at Billy Langford, he said, "We've got business to do. Who's coming with me?"

Billy, pale and drawn, shook his head. Zeke looked around the group. One by one they turned away. Finally he got to Mr. Carter. "Well?"

I could see Mr. Carter thinking about it. Next to him, Crawford was thinking too. He straightened his shoulders and turned to Mr. Carter.

"This is wrong," said Crawford. "You know it is."

Mr. Carter stared at him. Crawford stared right back. Finally Mr. Carter looked away. He said in a low voice, "Let's go home, boys. Maybe we'd best forget about this."

The men got to their feet and headed for the door. Billy Langford glanced at me and started to say something, then dropped his gaze and followed them out. Zeke didn't move.

Mr. Carter said, "I'll take that rope."

Zeke glared at him for the longest time. Then he handed the rope to Mr. Carter.

"You're not going to do anything foolish, are you?" said Mr. Carter.

"Not tonight," said Zeke. He turned and left.

TWENTY-FIVE

I went back up Market Street, by myself this time. The wind had died down, and the moon was shining out from behind the clouds. I wanted nothing more than to go home and climb in bed, but there was something else I had to do.

The lights were on at Dr. Morgan's house, but the black Ford was gone. Wondering if anyone was home, I opened the gate and made my way to the porch. As I drew near, I heard the sound of piano music and recognized it as a Beethoven sonata, one of Mama's favorites. The music was slow and mournful, sad but somehow comforting.

I stood there for a moment, just listening. Ludwig van Beethoven had been dead for almost a hundred years, and yet there he was, standing beside me in Dr. Morgan's front yard.

Through the screen door I saw the silhouette of a man at the piano, nodding as he played. He turned to one side, and the light revealed a craggy face, a large nose, and the stub of a cigar. It was H. L. Mencken.

He finished the sonata and sat motionless for a moment. Then he took the cigar from his mouth, poured himself a drink, and sipped it thoughtfully. Stepping onto the porch, I knocked.

Mencken looked up and came to the door. "Well, hello there, Monkey Girl." His voice was softer than usual, and there was a weary smile on his face. "Would you like to come in?"

"Yes, sir, if it's all right."

He led me into the parlor. "Can I get you some iced tea?" he asked.

"No, thank you."

He said, "Kent and Duffy went out driving somewhere. I decided I'd rather spend the evening with my friend Ludwig."

Taking a platter from the piano top, he offered it to me and said, "I was amazed to find that Dayton has a German bakery. Have you tried their strudel?"

I took one and bit into it. The taste of butter and apples filled my mouth.

"Strudel and Beethoven," he said. "My idea of a perfect evening."

He settled onto the piano bench, and I sat down next to him.

"I didn't know you liked music," I said.

"I don't like it. I live it. I inhale it. If it weren't for music, I would have killed myself long ago."

"Really?"

He said, "Ask my friends. We call ourselves the Saturday Night Club. Each time I'm at the point of shooting myself, Saturday night rolls around and I'm good for another week. We gather at someone's house to drink beer and play music—Beethoven, Brahms, Bach. Any of them are fine, so long as they're German."

He eyed me through his cigar smoke. "Are you German?"

"I don't think so."

"Pity," he said. He took a sip of his drink and stared off into the distance.

"Do you have a minute to talk?" I asked.

"I thought that's what we were doing."

"Some people are pretty mad at you," I said.

"My dear girl, I'd be disappointed if they weren't."

"No, I mean *really* mad. There's talk of beating you up, or even worse."

He cocked his head. "If I didn't know better, I'd say you were worried about me."

"They were planning to come here tonight. One of the men wanted to kill you."

"Oh?"

"This isn't a joke," I said. "I think you should leave town."

"All right," he said.

"Huh?"

"I'm planning to go home tomorrow after the trial," said Mencken. "Work is piling up at my office. Besides, I got a tip that Judge Raulston won't allow any more scientists to testify. If it's true, the case is over."

"But it just started."

"Justice is swift," he said. "As it turns out, so is injustice."

He turned back to the piano and played a series of soft chords. He finished, leaving only the sound of the crickets and the breeze.

"You remind me of someone," he said.

"Joe Mendi?"

He chuckled. "I was thinking of a friend of mine, Miss Sara Haardt. She lives in Baltimore but was born in Montgomery, Alabama. Sometimes she sits next to me at the piano, just like you're doing. I play music. She listens. We talk. I love the sound of her sweet, Southern voice."

"I thought you hated the South."

"Miss Robinson," he said, "the world is a more complicated place than you can possibly imagine."

He picked up a letter from the top of the piano. It was written in lovely, looping script and smelled faintly of lavender. "She's been under the weather, so she went to visit her family in Montgomery. It's hot there, too."

"And I remind you of her?"

"You don't always agree with me," he said. "I like that."

He set the letter down, then placed the stub of his cigar in an ashtray and took a fresh one from a box nearby. He clipped off the end, struck a match, and puffed the cigar until the tip glowed.

I said, "Are you and Miss Sara . . ."

"What?"

"Are you sweethearts?"

He squinted at me through the smoke. "Do I look like a sweetheart?" Removing his cigar, he took a sip of his drink. "I'm a bachelor and likely to remain so."

"You live by yourself?"

"Well, no, there's my mother," he said. "She's been sick too. To tell you the truth, I'm worried about her."

I stared at him. "Your mother? H. L. Mencken lives with his mother?"

"No. She lives with me."

A grin slowly spread across my face. "The reason you're going home isn't because of business. It's because you miss your mother!"

"That's ridiculous."

"You're just too embarrassed to admit it."

He said, "What makes you so sure? Oh, that's right, you live in Dayton. You people know everything." Heaving himself to his feet, he walked to the screen door and gazed outside.

"Why do you write such hurtful things?" I asked. "Do you enjoy it?"

"I just tell the truth," he said.

"No, you don't. You take the facts and twist them around to make people laugh. Mr. Bryan's not a buffoon. We're not imbeciles. Dayton's a nice town, full of nice people. That's not very exciting, but it's true."

Mencken shook his head. "Lord, save me from 'nice.'"

"You've hurt people. You've hurt our whole town. You've hurt my father."

"How do crickets make so much noise?" he said. "I've heard street construction that wasn't this loud."

He walked back to the piano, sat down, and began to play Bach. I didn't know the name of the piece, but I had heard Mama perform it many times. It was odd to hear music so delicate flowing from H. L. Mencken's rough hands. He grunted as he played, and flakes of cigar ash fell on the piano keys.

When he finished, he sipped his drink, then held out the glass and looked at it. "I exaggerate," he said. "What I write is truth magnified, truth distilled, like a good whiskey."

"I thought whiskey was illegal."

"You can still find it, even in Dayton," he said.

He tapped his cigar ash and looked at me. "Do you like grits?"

"What's that got to do with it?"

"Grits are the blandest food in creation. They taste like library paste. But Miss Sara taught me something very interesting. If you add cheese and garlic, they're delicious. That's the way it is with the truth. You can offer it up bland, or you can add a dash of criticism and exaggeration. Season to taste and serve."

I said, "I was taught that if it's not true, it's a lie."

"If only life were that simple," said Mencken. He turned back to the keyboard and began to play.

"I know that piece," I said. "It's the *Moonlight Sonata*."

He looked at me, surprised. "Do you play?"

"A little. Mama's teaching me."

"Let's do it together," he said. "You play the right hand and I'll play the left."

He started the slow, rolling notes, his tobacco-stained fingers pressing the keys firmly yet gently. Until that instant I had heard the beauty in those notes but never the sadness. When I joined in a moment later, H. L. Mencken leaned back and closed his eyes. Studying his face, I saw no sign of the wisecracking journalist who'd been wandering the streets of Dayton. I realized this must be the face that Miss Sara gazed at when she sat next to him at the piano.

I looked at our two hands, one large and one small, one rough and one smooth, as different as two hands could be. They moved together, tracing Beethoven's path across the keyboard.

The music floated over the piano, shimmering like a ribbon, then fluttered off into the night.

TWENTY-SIX

J ust as H. L. Mencken had predicted, Judge Raulston ruled on Friday that no more scientific testimony would be allowed. Clarence Darrow and the other defense lawyers complained bitterly, but the judge wouldn't change his mind. At ten thirty in the morning, just an hour and a half after beginning, Raulston adjourned the court until Monday.

I learned this at ten forty-five, when people from the trial began arriving at the store. I had been there since eight, working beside my father. Billy Langford had come in at nine and pulled me aside.

"Are you going to tell your father?" asked Billy. His eyes were red. There were lines on his face that I hadn't seen before.

I glared at him. "Did you really do all those things?" I demanded. "The Mansion? Myrna Maxwell? The tips to that photographer?"

He nodded. There was an expression on his face halfway between shame and pride.

"Billy," I said, trying to control myself, "what were you thinking?"

"I wanted to help Dayton. Your father brought the trial here, and I was going to make sure we won."

"'We'?" I said. "What about Johnny Scopes? Isn't he part of this town? How could you treat him like that? You've made his life miserable."

Billy didn't answer.

"And H. L. Mencken?" I said. "My God, he could have been killed."

"I know," said Billy, a stricken look on his face. "I was just trying to get some publicity, like your father did."

"Did you ever think that my father might have been wrong? He's not perfect. Haven't you noticed that most of the publicity Dayton's getting is bad?"

Billy stared at me. I could tell he would have to think about that one for a while.

"Hey, you two, get a move on," Daddy called from across the room. "We have customers."

"Yes, sir!" replied Billy. Turning back to me, he said, "You won't tell, will you?" He looked at me, pleading. "I made a mistake. Things got out of hand."

Billy wasn't the only one who had let things get out of hand. I thought of how I had started out having doubts about my father and somehow had ended up suspecting him of things he would never do.

"No," I said. "I won't tell him."

Billy blinked quickly a couple of times. "Thank you, Frances. You won't regret this."

We went back to work, and at about eleven o'clock Clarence Darrow entered the store with Reverend Charles Potter, a Unitarian preacher from New York. I waited on their table and was surprised to hear them discussing Bible passages.

". . . while you're at it," Darrow was saying, "look for the unscientific parts, like Joshua making the sun stand still. Type them up and get them to me by tomorrow this time. I might want to use some of them."

"Would you like to order?" I said.

"Yes, indeed," said Darrow, turning to face me. "Two Coca-Colas and a couple of those fancy sandwiches. What are they called again?"

"You mean the ham special?"

"That's it."

He turned back to Potter, and as I wrote down their order, I heard Darrow say in a low voice, "They think they've won the trial, but I've got a surprise for them. On Monday I'm planning to put a Bible expert on the stand. No, not you—a greater expert than you, the greatest expert in the world. This thing isn't over yet."

I walked away, grinning. Johnny still had a chance to win! I pictured the jury announcing that he was innocent. I would shake his father's hand, then run up and give Johnny a big hug. I might even kiss him, at least on the cheek.

I wanted to tell Johnny what I'd heard, but he had left town for the weekend with his father. Then I thought of someone else who would want to know.

I turned the order in to Daddy and said, "Could I leave for a few minutes? I have to go talk to somebody."

"Right now? The lunch crowd will be here soon."

"This won't take long. Please, Daddy? It's important."

He looked at his watch. "All right. But be back by eleven thirty."

"Yes, sir."

Whipping off my apron, I put it behind the counter and hurried out of the store. I raced up Main Street to Market and on to Dr. Morgan's house. When I knocked on the door, Edmund Duffy answered.

"Hello, Frances," he said, smiling. "I haven't seen you for a few days."

I said, "Is Mr. Mencken here?"

"Well, no. He's gone."

"Gone where?" I asked.

"Home. Kent's driving him to Chattanooga to catch a train. They just left."

I'm not sure why I was so disappointed. If I had convinced Mencken to stay, he probably would have written more nasty things about Dayton. He might even have gotten hurt. Maybe what I'd really wanted was to just see him again before he left, to study his face and talk to him about the *Moonlight Sonata*.

Ed said, "Sorry you missed him. But he did leave something for you. Come on in."

I followed Ed into the parlor, where he picked up an envelope from the piano and handed it to me. On the outside Mencken had written "Frances Robinson." Inside was a handwritten note.

Dear Monkey Girl,

I didn't want to leave without saying good-bye, but I had a chance to catch an earlier train to Baltimore and decided to take it. I shudder to think of the stack of papers waiting for me on my desk.

Please tell the town fathers, including yours, that I won't be able to accept the key to the city after all. I know they'll be disappointed.

I can't say I'll miss your town. However, I will miss T. T. Martin, the apple strudel, and the late-evening piano duets. It's sobering to think that after spending a week here I've made just two friends—a little girl and a raving lunatic. I can't decide whether that says more about me or about Dayton.

I enjoyed sharing Beethoven with you. It saddens me to think that most people don't even know who he is. Then again, maybe it's good. If they knew, there probably would be a movement to condemn his work. Baptist clergymen would speak out against it, and somebody would pass a law. In the end some poor musician would be put on trial for playing it and ridden out of town on a rail.

*The world is a terrible and beautiful place, Monkey Girl.
I'm happy to have shared your corner of it for a few days.*

*Your friend,
H. L. Mencken*

As it turned out, H. L. Mencken did leave too soon. Judge Raulston may have prevented the scientists from testifying, but there was one more person Clarence Darrow wanted to put on the stand. It was the last person you'd ever expect. His appearance was a bombshell, and the shock waves traveled over the radio, through the telegraph wires, and around the world.

TWENTY-SEVEN

Business had slowed down at Robinson's over the weekend, so I got permission from Daddy to take Monday off from the store. I wondered what Clarence Darrow had planned. If he was going to show that Johnny was innocent, I wanted to be in the front row.

That's exactly where I sat, thanks again to Mr. Scopes. As I settled in next to him and studied his profile, I realized that this was what Johnny would look like in forty years.

I imagined an older Johnny sitting on a porch at the end of the day, rocking and fanning himself. I pictured myself beside him, holding his hand, pouring him a glass of iced tea. We would watch the sunset and talk about our life together—the day we met, our courtship and marriage, our first house, our children. I would stroke his cheek, and he would smile. His skin would no longer be smooth, but he would still be the handsomest man in Dayton.

As always, we would talk about the trial and how it had brought us together. The trial had started off badly, but, thanks to the brilliant last-minute strategy of Clarence

Darrow, Johnny had won. He had stayed on at Rhea Central High School, and a few years later I had joined him on the faculty. The rest could be found on the pages of our family scrapbooks.

The sharp crack of a gavel dissipated my thoughts like so much smoke. As my vision cleared, I saw Judge Raulston's stern expression and the disapproving looks the jurors gave to Clarence Darrow. For the first time, it hit me that Johnny might lose the trial. Worse, I might lose Johnny.

Suddenly the porch, the smile, the sunset, the scrapbook—all of it seemed like a little girl's dream. The jurors wanted Johnny to lose. So did the crowd. The only thing standing between Johnny and a guilty verdict was some obscure trick that Darrow had up his tattered sleeve. I leaned forward, waiting to find out what it was.

I didn't find out that morning, unless Darrow's strategy was to put the jury to sleep. One of his lawyers read from a science textbook and then from letters that had been written by eight different scientists. When court adjourned for lunch, I invited Johnny and Mr. Scopes across the street for sandwiches at my house. Mama made up a big batch of iced tea, which surely tasted good after the heat of the courtroom.

While we ate, Mama asked, "How are you feeling about the trial these days, Johnny?"

"To tell you the truth, ma'am, I'll be glad when it's over," he said.

"Not me," said Mr. Scopes. "It's been a grand adventure. I wouldn't have missed it for the world."

"What if they find you guilty?" I asked Johnny.

"It could happen," he said. "And if it does, the whole world will know it."

Mr. Scopes grunted. "Don't give up, lad. Mr. Darrow isn't done yet."

After lunch we returned to the courthouse, where Judge Raulston had an unexpected announcement. There was a report that cracks had been discovered in the ceiling below the courtroom, and the county commissioners were concerned about damage from the weight of the crowd. As a result the afternoon session would have to be moved.

I couldn't imagine where else the trial could be held. It had been hard enough choosing the courthouse to start with. What other building in town could be used? Other people must have wondered the same thing, because they began to talk among themselves. The judge pounded his gavel and finished the announcement. The trial would be moved outside, onto the wooden speaker's platform that had been built on the courthouse lawn.

The crowd buzzed. Old Mr. Scopes grinned at me. "There's a circus on that lawn, with monkeys and more than a few clowns. Now the trial's going to be part of it. When you think about it, lass, it's the perfect ending."

The spectators spilled out of the courtroom, down the stairs, and onto the lawn. Tables and chairs were set up on the platform, and people pushed and shoved to get a good view. As word spread, the preachers moved in, trying to score a few points and win some converts. The vendors followed, selling everything from cream soda to hula skirts. Behind them came a sea of people, shouting and laughing, whooping and hollering, stretching into the distance as far as you could see.

Judge Raulston mounted the platform and took a seat behind one of the tables, with the court reporter next to him and the lawyers surrounding him on wooden benches. The twelve jurors sat off to one side. News reporters and spectators jammed in close, some of them on the platform and the rest seated on the grass. Old Mr. Scopes and I found a spot at the foot of the steps, where we had a good view of everything.

"Hold on tight," said Mr. Scopes. "It may be a wild ride."

I had been wondering all morning about Clarence Darrow's secret strategy. Who was the Bible expert he had mentioned at Robinson's? Wouldn't a Bible expert be better for Bryan's side than for Darrow's? And what could Darrow possibly hope to accomplish by bringing out the expert at the very end of the trial?

The answer to those questions turned out to be the most remarkable part of the trial, the part people would talk about for years and years to come.

Judge Raulston pounded his gavel, and one of the

defense lawyers rose to make an announcement. It struck like a thunderbolt.

"The defense," he said, "calls William Jennings Bryan as a witness."

The crowd broke out in an excited hubbub. The reporters looked at each other, amazed. A prosecution lawyer testifying for the defense? No one had ever heard of such a thing.

Grinning, I turned to Mr. Scopes. "Mr. Darrow said he was going to call the world's greatest Bible expert as a witness. I guess now we know who that is."

Mr. Scopes said, "I knew it! Mr. Darrow's not going down without a fight."

The prosecution lawyers didn't like it one bit. They leaped to their feet, shouting objections. I guess they figured that whatever Darrow had in mind, it couldn't be good.

Judge Raulston, in the middle of all the commotion, seemed confused and unsure of what to do. Bryan settled it by jumping to his feet.

"Where do you want me to sit?" he declared.

"Mr. Bryan," said Raulston, "you are not objecting to going on the stand?"

Bryan replied, "Not at all."

The Great Commoner strode to the witness chair and sat down, fanning himself. He wore a white shirt with a black bow tie, and striped trousers. His bald head was ringed with sweat, which he wiped periodically with a handkerchief from his pocket. Across from him stood Clarence Darrow, dressed in a wrinkled shirt with purple suspenders.

The judge asked Darrow, "Do you want Mr. Bryan sworn?"

Darrow smiled amiably. "No, I take it you will tell the truth, Mr. Bryan."

Bryan nodded, and the crowd yelled their approval. At last, after seven days of speeches, many of them technical and boring, the people were going to get what they had been hoping for since the beginning of the trial: a showdown between Clarence Darrow and William Jennings Bryan.

The people were eager to see it, and so was I. I desperately wanted Johnny Scopes to be found innocent. But for me it was more than that. For the past two months I'd been torn in half, part of me wanting the world to stay as it was and the other part itching to change it. Part of me believed the Bible, and part believed the scientists. Part of me trusted Daddy, and part saw a stranger. Part of me loved Dayton, and part thought it was Monkey Town.

Seeing Bryan and Darrow together on that elevated stage, eyeing each other while the crowd roared, I wondered if at last things would become clear. The two halves of me were facing off, sizing each other up, choosing weapons. And the whole world looked on.

Darrow turned to Bryan. "You have given considerable study to the Bible, haven't you, Mr. Bryan?"

"Yes, sir, I have tried to," Bryan replied. "I have studied the Bible for about fifty years, or some time more than that."

Bryan was calm, assured, confident. He smiled at the crowd. These were his people, and the Bible was his subject. What could Darrow possibly hope to gain?

Darrow said, "Do you claim that everything in the Bible should be literally interpreted?"

"I believe everything in the Bible should be accepted as it is given there," said Bryan.

"For example," said Darrow, "when you read that Jonah was swallowed by a whale, do you believe that?"

"I believe in a God who can make a whale, and can make a man, and can make both do what he pleases," said Bryan.

The crowd cheered, and part of me did too. Darrow didn't blink. "Perfectly easy to believe that Jonah was swallowed by a whale?"

"If the Bible said so," Bryan replied.

Darrow went on. "Do you believe Joshua made the sun stand still?" he asked.

Bryan said, "I accept the Bible absolutely."

"The Bible says Joshua commanded the sun to stand still for the purpose of lengthening the day, doesn't it, and you believe it?"

"I do."

Darrow cocked his head, pretending to be surprised. "Oh, really? You believe that at that time the sun went around the earth?"

"Well, no," said Bryan. "I believe that the earth goes around the sun."

For a moment Bryan was confused, and so was I. What was Darrow getting at?

Darrow said, "So, if the day was lengthened by stopping either the earth or the sun, it must have been the earth?"

"Well," Bryan answered, "I should say so."

"Mr. Bryan, have you ever pondered what would have happened to the earth if it had stood still? Don't you know it would have been converted into a molten mass of matter?"

"The God I believe in could have taken care of that, Mr. Darrow."

"You have never investigated that subject?" said Darrow.

"I have been too busy on things I thought were of more importance than that," Bryan said.

The crowd cheered again, but not so loudly this time.

Darrow picked up a Bible and opened it to a place he had marked. "Let's talk for a moment about Noah's ark and the Great Flood. You believe the story of the Flood to be a literal interpretation?"

"Yes, sir."

"When was that flood?"

"I never made a calculation," said Bryan.

"What do you think?" asked Darrow.

"I do not think about things I don't think about."

Darrow asked, "Do you think about things you *do* think about?"

Bryan smiled sheepishly. "Well, sometimes," he said.

There was nervous laughter in the audience. The judge called out, "Order!"

I looked over at Johnny. He was leaning forward, listening intently. In his eyes I saw something that hadn't been there for days: hope. My feelings might be at stake, but for Johnny it was his entire future.

A. T. Stewart, one of Bryan's lawyers, stood up and said, "I want to object, Your Honor. I do not think the defendant has a right to conduct the examination any further, and I ask Your Honor to exclude it."

Bryan gestured toward Darrow and the other defense attorneys. "These gentlemen did not come here to try this case. They came here to try revealed religion. I am here to defend it, and they can ask me any question they please."

Darrow smiled. Stewart shook his head and sat down. Judge Raulston turned to Darrow and said, "All right."

The audience, eager to hear more, clapped and cheered. Darrow looked out over the crowd and observed, "Great applause from the bleachers."

"From those whom you call 'yokels,'" said Bryan.

"I have never called them yokels."

Bryan insisted, "Those are the people you insult."

Darrow's eyes blazed. "You insult every man of science and learning in the world because he does not believe in your fool religion."

Stewart leaped to his feet again. "This has gone beyond the pale of a lawsuit, Your Honor. Mr. Darrow is making an effort to insult the gentleman on the witness stand, and I ask that it be stopped."

Raulston answered grimly, "To stop it now would not be just to Mr. Bryan. He wants to answer the questions. Proceed, Mr. Darrow."

It was obvious the prosecution team was worried. Darrow, having gained the advantage, hammered home his questions like nails.

"Do you think the earth was made in six days?" he asked Bryan.

"Not six days of twenty-four hours."

"Doesn't it say so?" asked Darrow.

"No, sir."

Darrow leaned forward. "You think those were not literal days?"

"My impression is they were periods."

"Have you any idea of the length of the periods?" Darrow asked.

"No, I don't."

Darrow said, "Now, if you call those periods, they may have been a very long time."

"They might have been," Bryan admitted.

"The Creation might have been going on for a very long time?"

Bryan said, "It might have continued for millions of years."

It was just one brief statement, but for me it opened the door a crack, and light came streaming in. For the past week Bryan had been saying that the Bible and evolution don't mix—if you believe in one, you can't believe in the other. But if creation happened over millions of years, then his statement was no longer true. It would be possible to believe in the Bible and evolution at the same time. Evolution, like creation, could have taken place in seven days, if the days were long enough. And it wasn't Clarence Darrow who had said so; it was William Jennings Bryan.

All this time I had assumed that I needed to believe one side or the other. Darrow, Mencken, even Johnny Scopes himself—if they were right, then my father and the town of Dayton must be wrong. But it didn't have to be that way. Maybe all of them were right, and all of them were wrong. Maybe each was a little bit right. Maybe I could look at the world and decide for myself. It didn't have to be right for Daddy or Johnny or Eloise Purser or Clarence Darrow, only for me.

A calm settled over me, the first I had felt in weeks. But

Darrow wasn't through. "Mr. Bryan," he said, "do you believe that the first woman was Eve?"

"Yes."

"Do you believe she was literally made out of Adam's rib, and that Adam, Eve, and their children were the only people on earth?"

"I do."

Darrow asked, "Then did you ever discover where her son Cain got his wife?"

"Beg your pardon?" said Bryan.

"The Bible says he got a wife, doesn't it? Were there other people on the earth at the time?"

"I cannot say."

"Well, where did she come from?" asked Darrow.

Bryan dismissed the question with a wave of his hand. "I leave the agnostics to hunt for her."

The crowd hooted, confident that Bryan was winning. I wasn't so sure.

"Do you believe the story of the temptation of Eve by the serpent?" asked Darrow.

"I do."

"And you believe," said Darrow, "that God made the serpent to go on his belly after he tempted Eve?"

Bryan said, "I believe that."

"Have you any idea how the snake went before that time?"

"No, sir."

"Do you know whether he walked on his tail or not?" asked Darrow.

The audience laughed, but Bryan didn't think it was funny. "Your Honor," he said, "I think I can shorten this testimony. The only purpose Mr. Darrow has is to slur the Bible."

The crowd cheered. Darrow yelled over the uproar, "I object to your statement. I am exempting you on your fool ideas that no intelligent Christian on earth believes."

His words brought a round of boos. People leaped to their feet, yelling angrily. On the speaker's platform, Johnny stood up and looked out defiantly at the crowd. They pushed forward so Mr. Scopes and I were pressed up against the steps.

Mr. Scopes glanced nervously at the crowd. "If this keeps up, someone could get hurt."

The angry crowd pushed in closer. There were shouted threats. Dayton was about to explode, right there in front of the whole world.

Suddenly there was a loud *crack!* I saw Judge Raulston standing above the crowd, gripping his gavel like a weapon. He pounded it on the table again and again.

"Silence!" he roared. "Silence!"

The crowd hesitated. Judge Raulston stepped forward and bellowed, "Court is adjourned until nine o'clock tomorrow morning."

The police moved in quickly, and the crowd began to

disperse. Mr. Scopes turned to me. "I'd say that was a close one."

I thought about what we had just seen—the angry crowd, the tough questions, the big showdown between Darrow and Bryan—and I wondered what could possibly come next.

"It has to end soon, doesn't it?" I said.

Mr. Scopes took out a handkerchief and wiped his forehead. "Aye, lass," he said. "Otherwise, I swear we'll all melt into a great big puddle."

I said, "Now that we know Darrow's secret strategy, do you think it worked?"

"The only people who know," said Mr. Scopes, "are those twelve men."

He nodded toward the jurors, who were filing down the steps next to us. I studied their faces for clues about a verdict. Would they go along with the rest of the town and vote against Johnny? Or would they step out of the crowd, weigh the facts, and decide for themselves? If I could do it, maybe they could too.

TWENTY-EIGHT

I woke up Tuesday morning to the sound of rain. Slipping out of bed, I pulled my robe around me and went to the window. I opened it and was amazed to feel a cool breeze. Finally, after weeks of blazing sunshine, the heat had broken.

At breakfast I got Daddy's permission to attend the trial for what surely would be the last day. I practiced the piano for a while, then at eight-thirty gathered up my things and said good-bye to Mama.

"Don't forget to take an umbrella," she said.

I met old Mr. Scopes at the courthouse steps, where he explained that Judge Raulston had moved the trial back inside because of the rain.

"It will mean a smaller crowd," said Mr. Scopes, "but there should be plenty of action."

On Monday the trial had ended with William Jennings Bryan on the witness stand. Everyone expected it to start that way on Tuesday. I was hoping that Clarence Darrow would have more time questioning Bryan, to help convince the jury that evolution wasn't so terrible so that Johnny might be found innocent.

But Judge Raulston had other ideas. First, he announced that Bryan would not be allowed to testify anymore. His next words surprised everyone.

"I feel that the testimony of Mr. Bryan can shed no light upon any issues that will be pending before the higher courts. The question is very simple: whether or not Mr. Scopes taught that man descended from a lower order of animals. And so, taking this view of it, I am pleased to expunge the testimony given by Mr. Bryan yesterday from the records of this court, and it will not be further considered."

I turned to old Mr. Scopes. "What does that mean?"

He said, "Bryan's testimony yesterday will be erased, as if it never happened. Which means that Johnny just lost his best chance to win. If the trial is about whether evolution contradicts the Bible, then it's Darrow against Bryan, and some of the jury might vote for Darrow. But if the only question is whether Johnny taught evolution in class—well, lass, no one denies that, not even Darrow himself."

Clarence Darrow rose to his feet. I had no doubt that he would object. After all, he was Johnny's defense lawyer.

Darrow said, "I think to save time we will ask the court to bring in the jury and instruct them to find the defendant guilty."

I turned to Mr. Scopes. "Doesn't he mean innocent? I thought he was on Johnny's side."

Mr. Scopes stared grimly ahead. "So did I. It appears that Mr. Darrow cares more about his precious cause than he does about Johnny."

"I don't understand," I said. "What cause?"

"Evolution. Teaching science in school. Now that Darrow realizes he can't win, he wants a verdict of guilty. That way he can appeal the verdict to higher courts, maybe even the Supreme Court. So Johnny pays the price, and Darrow gets more publicity for his cause."

"So if Johnny wins, Darrow loses. And if Johnny loses, Darrow wins."

"Aye, lass. It's not about justice. It's all about publicity."

Publicity—I was sick of that word. Daddy had wanted it, and Dayton had suffered. Billy Langford had wanted it, and there was a lynch mob. Now Darrow wanted it, and Johnny Scopes, the man who had just been trying to help, lost his last defender.

The jury was brought in, and Judge Raulston, Stewart, and Darrow spent most of the morning informing them of their duty. Finally, Judge Raulston instructed them to ignore all the arguments about whether the theory of evolution was correct. Instead, they should focus on just one issue.

"If you find that the defendant did teach that man descended from a lower order of animals," Raulston told them, "then the defendant would be guilty and should be so found."

It sounded simple, as if there were no way Johnny could be found innocent. Both sides agreed that he had taught evolution. Still, I kept thinking about the twelve jurors. Surely there was one who had some doubts. That was all we needed. One vote, and Johnny's name could still be cleared.

The jury left the room at eleven fifteen. As they filed out, I closed my eyes and did something Johnny Scopes would never do. Clarence Darrow wouldn't do it either, not that I cared two figs for him.

I prayed.

"God," I said under my breath, "it's been a long time since we talked. I've been kind of busy, with the trial and all. Plus, some people around here don't seem too sure about whether you're even there. I think you are. But I don't agree with Mr. Bryan. I don't think you fit in some little box or between the covers of a book. You're bigger than that, aren't you? I hope so, because I need you to help Johnny. I love him. Don't laugh. I know something about love, even if I am only fifteen. God, won't you please talk to those jurors? Maybe some of them are Baptists, but they still believe in you. Give them a nudge. Tell them he's innocent. Tell them he's a good man and doesn't deserve this. Won't you please do that for me, God? Thank you. Yours truly, Frances Robinson. Amen."

The jury came back at eleven twenty-four, just nine minutes later.

Raulston said, "Mr. Foreman, will you tell us whether you have agreed on a verdict?"

"Yes, sir," said the jury foreman. "We have found the defendant guilty."

Maybe my prayer hadn't been good enough. Maybe there wasn't a God to answer it. Or maybe praying, like so many other things I learned about that summer, was more complicated than I had thought it was.

With the jury's announcement, excited chatter broke out in the audience. Several reporters raced from the room, heading for the telegraph office.

Judge Raulston called for order, then declared that Johnny would pay a one-hundred-dollar fine. He pounded his gavel and announced, "This court is hereby adjourned."

After all the preparation and excitement and visitors and words and words and words—millions of them, by the lawyers and witnesses and reporters from around the world—the trial finally was over. Johnny Scopes was guilty.

I wanted to go to him and tell him it was okay. I wanted to say that those people didn't know him the way I did, that he was a fine person and nothing could change that. I wanted to say that I loved him. But the reporters came between us. They gathered around him, shouting out questions, pushing him farther and farther away. The world had him now, and I wondered if I would ever get him back. As he disappeared into the crowd, I realized that I was crying.

I looked around and saw a familiar figure standing in the doorway. It was Mama. Wiping my eyes, I made my way over to her and asked, "What are you doing here?"

She put her arm around my shoulders. "I decided that I wanted to see some history too," she said.

We went down the stairway and out the front door. The rain had stopped and the sun was shining. We stood on the courthouse lawn, soaking in the carnival atmosphere for perhaps the last time.

I said, "He never had a chance, did he?"

"No, he didn't," said Mama.

"I actually thought he could win. I thought Clarence Darrow would defend him."

"It wasn't about John Scopes," she said. "It never was."

I said, "I guess I'm pretty naive."

"You're a good girl," said Mama.

"I'd rather be a good woman."

"You will be soon enough. Too soon for my taste."

I said, "Mama, I need to tell you something."

"What's that?"

"I broke my promise. I said I'd never lie to you again, but I did."

She studied my face. "Go on."

"Remember the night you were making cookies, and I asked if I could go to Eloise's house? Well, I didn't go. Eloise and I went into town. There was trouble, and she needed help. I was going to tell you, but Eloise didn't want me to. She said if I didn't help, she'd go by herself. She was scared."

Mama said, "I see."

"So I lied. I'm really sorry, but that's what I did. She's my friend. I thought it was the only thing I could do."

"What was the trouble?" asked Mama.

I told her about the meeting at the hardware store, being careful not to mention Billy Langford. I described what the men were planning and how Eloise, Crawford, and I had helped to break it up.

"You stood up to Mr. Carter?" she said.

"Yes, but it was Crawford who stopped him. Crawford told him it was wrong."

She considered this for a moment. "Frances, do you realize what you've done?"

"Yes, ma'am. It won't happen again."

"That's not what I mean," she said. "You may have saved H. L. Mencken's life. Maybe you saved Dayton, too."

"Dayton? I don't understand."

"Think about it," she said. "The trial's given us a bad enough name as it is. Can you imagine what people would say if H. L. Mencken had been hurt? Can you imagine what *Mencken* would say? 'Yokels' would be the least of it. Lord, help us."

Mama looked me in the eye. "You lied, Frances, and I don't like it one bit. But you also did a good thing." The hint of a smile crossed her face. "It's confusing, isn't it?"

"Yes, ma'am."

She took my hand, and we headed home. Climbing the steps to our porch, we looked back at all the color and commotion on the courthouse lawn. It was hard to believe that in a few days it would be gone.

"It was all a big mistake, wasn't it," I said.

"Maybe," she said. "But you'll have some good stories to tell your children."

"It hurt Mr. Scopes. Daddy's the one who planned it."

"Don't be too hard on your father," she said. "He's a fine man. He has the best of intentions, even if things don't always work out. And he loves you desperately."

"He does?"

"When you're angry with him, you can't imagine how much it hurts. He's been miserable the past few days."

The thought of Daddy feeling bad about me seemed odd and somehow comforting.

I said, "He's not being fair to Mr. Scopes. He hasn't offered him a contract yet."

"Your father's not the only one involved. He has to follow the wishes of the school board. You have no idea how much pressure he's getting from them."

"That doesn't make it right," I said.

"I can't tell you very much about it," said Mama, "but I can say this much. Your father is Johnny's best friend on the board. He's trying to work things out. He's even made a few enemies, which is hard for someone like him."

"What do you think will happen?" I asked.

"I don't know. But he's doing his best. He needs your support."

I said, "He's different from the way I always thought he was."

"He hasn't changed," said Mama.

"I have."

"I know," she said.

TWENTY-NINE

The trial had ended just in time for lunch at Robinson's. That afternoon and for the next several days the prosecution lawyers claimed victory. The defense answered by saying that things had turned out just the way they had planned.

Everyone had an opinion, and we heard most of them. Sue Hicks and George Rappleyea staked out tables in the center of the store and, fortified by Coca-Colas, told their stories to anyone who would listen.

I got a Coca-Cola for myself and watched them. Sipping it, I thought it tasted different from before. It wasn't medicine. It was just a drink. There was something artificial about it, like the stories Sue was telling, like the publicity my father had dreamed up. I had to admit, though, it still tasted pretty good.

While Sue talked, the reporters huddled mysteriously in one corner of the store, like revolutionaries hatching a plot. The plot, it turned out, was a party to thank the people of Dayton for their hospitality. The reporters hired a band and rented the American Legion Hall, then invited everyone in town to attend, including the lawyers from both sides.

I was there, along with my family and just about everyone else in Dayton. As we arrived, Mama said, "I see someone you know."

Following her gaze, I spotted Eloise Purser fidgeting by the punch bowl, wearing a frilly blue dress that looked brand new.

Mama said, "She looks lonely, don't you think?"

I watched Eloise for a moment. Mama squeezed my hand, and I headed across the room. When I reached Eloise, she said, "Can I pour you some punch?"

I nodded, and she filled two glasses. We stood next to each other, neither of us knowing quite what to say, sucking down punch like there was no tomorrow. Across the room, Sonny saw us and began grinning and waving. I tried to ignore him.

I said to Eloise, "I like your dress."

She grinned sheepishly. "It itches."

"So does mine. You get used to it."

We drank more punch, and then I said, "I haven't seen you since that night at Dayton Hardware. I hope you didn't get in trouble."

"It wasn't so bad," she said. "When we got home, Crawford decided to tell my parents. They were mad at first, but then I told them what you and Crawford did. They said you did the right thing."

Eloise looked at me. "I couldn't believe you stood up to those men."

"So did Crawford," I said.

"Only because you did. That was the bravest thing I ever saw."

I glanced away but couldn't keep from smiling.

Eloise said, "I'm sorry I said those things about Mr. Scopes. You know, in court that day."

"You mean Johnny?" I said.

"I don't know why you call him that. He's a teacher."

"He's a wonderful man."

"Can I ask you something?" said Eloise. "Do you love him?"

Eloise and I hadn't been talking much lately, but she was still my best friend. If she didn't deserve to know, who did?

I said, "Yes, I do."

"That is so romantic," she said.

"I thought you didn't like him. He's an agnostic."

"Yes," she said, "but he's cute."

She giggled, and so did I. Somehow we couldn't stop. Pretty soon we were laughing so hard that I spilled my punch. When Eloise tried to pour me some more, she missed the glass and hit my shoe, which made us laugh even harder.

The festivities started soon after that. There were speeches and prizes, including a pair of chartreuse suspenders donated by Clarence Darrow and a silk shirt from Dudley Field Malone. Then the band played, and people streamed out onto the dance floor.

The lawyers had been yelling at each other for days, but watching them at the party you never would have known it. A. T. Stewart danced with Clarence Darrow's wife, and Darrow paired up with Mrs. Stewart. Doris Stevens whirled Judge Raulston around the floor in a Viennese waltz, then did the Charleston with Sue Hicks.

Johnny, who loved parties better than anybody, danced with Eloise and just about every other girl in the room except me. Finally, as I was about to give up, I turned around and there he was. He had taken off his coat and rolled up his sleeves like he used to do when I watched him at football practice, in another lifetime when he was just a coach and teacher.

"Come on, Frances," said Johnny, smiling. "Let's show them how it's done."

He spun me around the room until I was dizzy. People began to notice, and one by one they stepped back to watch until we were alone on the dance floor. By the end of the song Johnny was out of breath and his eyes were bright. The people applauded and Johnny grinned, looking as relaxed at the party as he had been nervous and uncomfortable in the courtroom.

The band began a slow number by George Gershwin, and Johnny offered me his hand. I took it, and he put his other hand on my waist.

Daddy had always loved to dance, and sometimes in the evenings he would show me a few steps in the parlor while Mama played the piano. I would close my eyes and relax, letting him lead me across the floor.

With Johnny it was different. It wasn't like dancing at all. It was like gliding across the sky. We moved around the floor, suspended above the other dancers, in our own little world.

I remembered that day at the Mansion—it seemed like years ago—when Johnny had taught me the monkey glide. I had pictured myself in a beautiful dress, dancing with him to a Gershwin song. At least one of my dreams had come true.

I said, "Did you ever wish something could go on and on forever?"

"I thought the trial would."

"I meant this dance. The music."

He shrugged. "I suppose so."

"Come on," I said, "the trial's over. Stop worrying about it."

Johnny shook his head. "You're wrong, Frances. For me it'll never really end."

There was such a sad look in his eyes. Without thinking, I pulled him close and stroked his hair, the way Mama sometimes did with me. Johnny rested his head on mine, and the music carried us around the dance floor.

On the other side of the room, I saw Daddy dancing with Mama. Their movements didn't seem as smooth as usual, and when I looked more closely I saw why. A few feet down, hugging their knees, Sonny was dancing along with them.

I studied Daddy's face. He wasn't a handsome man, but when he smiled, as he was doing now, just looking at him made me feel good.

When the music ended, I turned to Johnny. "Would you excuse me for a minute?" He nodded, and I crossed the floor to my family.

I tapped Daddy on the shoulder. "Could I have this dance?"

Mama reached down and picked up Sonny. "Come on, sweetheart," she told him, "let's you and me go get some punch."

They moved away, leaving Daddy and me on the dance floor. He held out his hand. I took it and stepped into his arms.

It didn't feel right at first. I was stiff and nervous. For the first few beats I tried to lead and ended up tripping over myself.

"Easy," he said. "Just relax."

I took a deep breath and closed my eyes. Gradually my steps lined up with his, and we began moving smoothly across the floor.

I opened my eyes. Daddy was watching me. There was a tender look in his eyes that I hadn't seen for a while. He said, "I didn't know if we'd ever do this again."

"I didn't either," I said. "It feels good."

"Are you still upset?"

I said, "Maybe a little."

"You know," he said, "I'm just a person. Just an ordinary man. Sometimes I stumble, like everybody else. I need you beside me when I do."

"You mean, I'm not supposed to disagree with you?"

"I didn't say that."

"Sometimes I have doubts," I said.

He grunted. "Seems to be a lot of that going around."

"You make it sound like a disease," I said. "Is it really so bad?"

"When I was a boy there was no such thing as doubt. The word didn't exist."

I said, "You also walked ten miles to school through snowdrifts as tall as a house."

"What happened to you, Frances? You used to believe everything I said."

I smiled. "I'm a little bit older, I guess."

"I'm a lot older," he said. "I wish I had a dime for every wrinkle I got during the trial. I'd be a wealthy man."

I said, "So, Daddy, who do you think was right?"

"At the trial? Lord, girl, do you have to ask?"

"I know you believe in the Bible," I said, "but you have to admit that Mr. Darrow said some interesting things."

"Clarence Darrow is a smart man who took a wrong

turn. How can a person live in this world and not believe in God?"

"Which God?" I said. "Mr. Bryan's or Dr. Metcalf's?"

"Who's Dr. Metcalf?"

"One of the scientists. He teaches Sunday school."

"Not at our church," said Daddy.

"Even Mr. Bryan admitted that creation could have taken millions of years."

Daddy cocked his head. "What are you saying?"

I shrugged, trying to act nonchalant. "I don't know. Maybe the evolutionists have a point."

Daddy stared at me. "You think we descended from monkeys?"

"Not necessarily."

"You think your Grandpa Haggard came swinging in on some tree?"

"That's not what I meant."

"Then maybe you can straighten me out," said Daddy.

"What I mean is, maybe both sides are right. God made the world in six days. We just don't know how long they were."

Daddy looked away. When he looked back, he said, "You've seen a lot over the past few weeks—probably more than a young girl should. Things are getting back to normal now. In a few days it'll seem like all of this never happened."

"You really think so?" I asked.

"Yes, I do."

"I'm not so sure."

Daddy said, "You may think those city folks are smart. But, sweetheart, they're different from us. They're loud. They're pushy. They don't say 'please' and 'thank you.' They have no idea how to make iced tea."

"I thought some of them were nice," I said. "And some of them weren't. Just like Dayton."

He looked at me with a funny expression on his face. "Are you growing up on me?"

I rested my head on his chest. "Nobody's all bad, no matter how awful they seem. Nobody's all good, either."

"Who are we talking about now?"

"I love you, Daddy. I know you're not perfect."

He said, "I guess my grand scheme didn't work out so well, did it? People learned about Dayton, but not the way I'd planned. Lord, what a mess."

"You didn't know," I said.

He chuckled. "We got some excitement, though, didn't we?"

"Yes, sir, we did."

The song ended, and the band struck up a fast number.

Daddy said, "This is where I came in. Let's go see how Sonny's doing with that punch."

"I'd like that," I said.

As we made our way across the floor, Daddy said,

"Frances, do me one favor. Don't tell your mama what you said about evolution. I'm afraid it would kill her."

"Funny," I told him, "that's what she said about you."

He laughed, and I did too. Then he put his arm around my shoulders, and we headed for the punch bowl.

THIRTY

After the trial, William Jennings Bryan decided to tour the area, visiting friends and making speeches. He returned to Dayton on Sunday morning, went to church, and ate dinner afterward. Then he lay down to take a nap and never woke up. Just five days after the trial ended, William Jennings Bryan was dead.

He had been staying at the Rogers' house, and within a few hours people started gathering outside. Some lit candles, some prayed, and some, like Daddy and me, just stood there gazing at the house, wondering how somebody so big and loud and colorful could blink out in his sleep like a lightbulb.

At breakfast the next morning I noticed that Mama seemed upset. She kept slamming drawers and dropping things, and finally she spilled a carton of eggs on the floor.

Daddy grabbed a dish towel and began mopping up the mess. "For heaven's sake, what's wrong?" he asked.

"It's that Mencken fellow," said Mama. She gestured

toward the Chattanooga paper, which was open on the counter. "See for yourself."

Daddy finished cleaning the floor, then put the dish towel in the sink and went over to look at the paper. I pulled up a step stool and peered over his shoulder. It was a long article, but the main idea was contained in a paragraph at the end:

Bryan was a vulgar and common man, a cad undiluted. He was ignorant, bigoted, self-seeking, blatant and dishonest. His career brought him into contact with the first men of his time; he preferred the company of rustic ignoramuses. It was hard to believe, watching him at Dayton, that he had traveled, that he had been received in civilized societies, that he had been a high officer of state. He seemed only a poor clod like those around him, deluded by a childish theology, full of an almost pathological hatred of all learning, all human dignity, all beauty, all fine and noble things. He was a peasant come home to the dung-pile. Imagine a gentleman, and you have imagined everything that he was not.

Daddy looked up from the newspaper, his face flushed with anger. "That's the most despicable thing I've ever read. The man's been dead less than a day, and already Mencken's gnawing on the corpse like a vulture."

While Daddy went on and on about the article, I read it again. I thought about the gentle musician I had come to know, and tried to imagine him writing these bitter, spiteful words. I couldn't do it.

Then again, I never could have imagined traffic jams on Market Street, a monkey in a tuxedo, worshippers babbling and twitching in the woods, or a lynch mob gathering at Dayton Hardware.

It was a different world from the one I had known two months ago. The best and worst of it had paraded past my front window, and I was still trying to make sense of it all. Maybe someday when I was older and wiser I would figure it out. Or maybe there was no sense to be made. A man fires off words like an assassin, then goes home, has a slice of apple strudel, and plays a Beethoven sonata.

"Eat your breakfast, Frances," said Mama.

"Yes, ma'am," I said.

I went back to the table, turned the lazy Susan, and took another biscuit.

People started to pack up and leave after that. On the courthouse lawn, vendors broke down booths and folded up tables. The Bible Champion of the World wandered around on his way out of town, challenging folks to match wits on Revelation and Deuteronomy.

Even T. T. Martin was leaving. I saw him at Robinson's the next morning, tossing down a chocolate soda while distributing religious pamphlets. He tried to give me one until he glanced up and saw my face.

He cocked his head and narrowed his eyes. "Haven't we met before?" he said.

I stuck out my tongue, and he grinned. "Ah, yes, Mr. Mencken's friend, the Monkey Girl. You know, I miss Henry. He came by to see me before leaving town."

"'Henry'?" I said. "Is that what you called him?"

Martin smiled wistfully. "He and I saw a lot of each other after that first day. I love a good argument, and he gave me all I could handle." He handed me a pamphlet, winked, and went on about his work.

At another table, Sue Hicks was posing for Ed Duffy. I brought Sue a Coca-Cola and set it down in front of him.

"Make sure to get this in your picture," I told Ed. "People won't recognize him without it."

Sue grinned. "She used to be such a nice girl," he said. "Then the trial came, and she's never been the same."

"Maybe that's not so bad," I said.

Ed flipped through his sketch pad and signed a page. Carefully tearing it from the pad, he handed it to me and said, "I'd like you to have this." It was the drawing of me from that day in the courtroom.

"Really? I can keep it?"

"Or sell it," said Ed. "Who knows, maybe it'll be worth something one day."

I studied the drawing. The girl in the picture really did

seem different. She looked older, especially around the eyes. I'm not exactly sure why. Maybe eyes change depending on what they've seen, like shoes picking up scratches and scuffs.

Johnny came by the store later that day. Daddy called him into the back room, and when they came out, Daddy shook Johnny's hand and said a few words to him. Johnny nodded, then came over to see me.

"Want to help me with something?" he asked.

"Sure. I'm just finishing up here."

I took off my apron and said something to Daddy, then followed Johnny outside, where his yellow roadster was parked at the curb. He reached into the backseat and pulled out a big overstuffed canvas bag and a metal can.

"What's in those?" I asked.

"You'll see."

Heaving the bag over his shoulder, he picked up the can and started down Main Street. I followed.

"What were you and Daddy talking about?" I asked.

"He offered me a job teaching at Rhea Central High School this fall."

"He did?" I said. "That's wonderful! That's perfect!"

I grinned up at Johnny, then looked past him at the pale blue sky. There wasn't a cloud in sight.

"I turned him down," Johnny said.

I stopped in my tracks. "What? Why?"

"Things wouldn't be the same."

"Of course they would," I said. "The trial's over."

He said, "For Dayton, maybe. For me, I don't think so. Anyway, it's time to move on."

"You mean, you're going to leave Dayton?"

"I'm afraid so," said Johnny. "You know, your father's offer wasn't the only one I got."

"What do you mean?" I asked.

He smiled mysteriously and started walking again. A few minutes later we reached an empty lot at the end of Main Street with a fire pit where people sometimes roasted hot dogs. Johnny set down the can and dropped the canvas bag. He untied the rope and dumped out the bag's contents. It had been filled with letters.

Kneeling, Johnny sifted through the letters and picked one out.

"'Dear Mr. Scopes,'" he read. "'I run a speakers' bureau in Hartford, Connecticut, and would be delighted to have you join our roster of world-famous personalities. I can offer you the sum of ten thousand dollars for five appearances.'"

I gasped. Johnny tossed the letter back into the pile and picked out another one. "'Dear Mr. Scopes: How would you like to make twenty-five thousand dollars in just six months?'"

Johnny looked up at me. "There are hundreds of these. Some are from colleges, some from vaudeville theaters, some even from circuses! It seems that everybody wants to hear me speak."

I stared at him. "Twenty-five thousand dollars just to stand up and talk?"

He said, "There's one from a movie company. They offered me fifty thousand."

"Fifty thousand dollars! And you can be in the movies? What are you going to do?"

"I'll show you," he said, climbing to his feet.

Johnny gathered up some branches and stacked them in the fire pit. Then, opening the can, he emptied it onto the stack.

"What is that?" I asked.

"Kerosene." He pulled a book of matches from his pocket and struck one. "Make a wish."

He dropped the match into the fire pit, and the branches exploded into flame. Taking a handful of letters, he tossed them into the fire pit.

"Come on, give me a hand," he said.

"You're sure you want to do this?" I asked.

"Absolutely."

I picked up some letters and very gingerly set them in the fire. I felt as if I were burning money.

"You can do better than that," said Johnny.

Grinning, he crouched over the pile and called out, "Hut! Hut!" Then he grabbed a handful of letters, took two quick steps backward, and hurled the letters into the pit, like a star quarterback on Friday night.

I remembered a game Sonny and I sometimes played in

the parlor, where we flipped playing cards, trying to make them lean up against the wall. I picked a letter from the pile and sent it spinning into the center of the flames.

"Good shot!" said Johnny.

He threw another pass, then picked up a long stick and began golfing letters into the pit. I joined him, and within a few minutes the pile of letters was gone.

Gazing at the flames, I said, "I can't believe we burned all of them."

"We didn't," said Johnny. He reached into his pocket and pulled out a carefully folded envelope.

Johnny said, "Some of the scientists who testified at the trial thought I might be out of a job, so they took up a collection for me to go back to school. I just got this letter from them, with a check to pay my tuition."

He took out the letter and handed it to me. It was signed by Dr. Maynard M. Metcalf and some other scientists.

"Have you decided where you'll go?" I asked.

He said, "At first I thought I might study law. Then I realized that if I did, every judge and lawyer I met would ask me about the Scopes trial. So I'll try something different. I'm going to the University of Chicago to study geology."

"You really are leaving?"

He nodded. "I'm all packed. I just wanted to say goodbye to my best friend in Dayton."

He leaned over and hugged me. I grabbed him around the waist and hung on for dear life.

"Bye, Johnny," I said. Then very softly I added, "I love you."

My voice was muffled against his chest, so I'm not sure he heard me. Just the same, it felt good to say the words.

When Johnny had lit the fire a few minutes earlier, he had said, "Make a wish." My wish had been a simple one: that someday he would love me as much as I loved him.

We watched the fire burn down, then covered up the ashes and headed back to Johnny's car. He packed up the last of his things and climbed in.

"So long, kiddo," he said. "Take care of yourself. Don't drink too much Coca-Cola." He ruffled my hair the way he used to. Somehow it didn't bother me today.

Then he started the engine, pulled out, and headed up the street. I watched the car until it was just a yellow speck, rising up toward the mountains and into the world.

AUTHOR'S NOTE

My friend Craig Gabbert always told me that his family was involved in the Scopes trial, but I had never thought much about it. Then, in the summer of 1994, Craig invited several friends, including my wife and me, to go with him and his family to the Scopes trial reenactment in Dayton, Tennessee.

It was hot that summer, as it had been in 1925, and when Craig introduced us to his mother, Frances Robinson Gabbert, she offered us a pitcher of iced tea. We sat sipping tea on the front porch of her house, gazing across the street at the Rhea County Courthouse and listening to her stories of seventy years before, when as a little girl she had witnessed one of the most remarkable events in American history. Her father, it turned out, had been F. E. Robinson, the "hustling druggist" of Dayton, at whose store the trial had been planned. The round oak table where we ate lunch that day was the same one where William Jennings Bryan and Clarence Darrow (but not H. L. Mencken) had been invited for supper during the Scopes trial.

The reenactment was fascinating, but the best part of that weekend was listening to Frances tell her stories. They seized my imagination, though for a while I wasn't sure what to do with them. I thought of approaching Frances about writing a memoir but never got around to it. Then, two years later, she died and the opportunity seemed lost.

But the stories wouldn't let go. I continued to roll them around in my mind, and more and more they began to sound like a novel. I could use Frances's stories, follow the outline of historical facts, and yet have the freedom to imagine scenes where there were gaps and write dialogue to bring the stories to life.

That's what I did. The resulting book, including research, took a year and a half to write and another few years to revise. Several characters, such as Billy Langford and Myrna Maxwell, are fictional, but nearly all the rest were real.

As for Frances, I like to think I've remained true to her spirit, but many of the facts were changed. To begin with, at the time of the trial she was eight years old, not fifteen, and in addition to her brother, Sonny, she had a sister named Andrewena, known to the family as Dee. Frances worshipped her father, and, according to everyone, they never experienced the kind of conflict I've described. It is fiction.

Frances knew John Scopes but, being eight years old, surely never had romantic feelings for him. He left Dayton before she was ten. Regarding H. L. Mencken, she never got to know him and in fact, along with the rest of Dayton, thought he was a horrible man. There was a group that threatened to lynch Mencken, but it wasn't Frances who broke it up; it was her grandfather, A. P. Haggard.

Billy Langford's plot to sabotage John Scopes and the defense team, like Billy himself, is fictional, though individual pieces of it, such as the lynch mob and the setup to photograph John Scopes kissing a woman, actually took place. Otherwise, virtually all the information is as accurate as I could make it in the context of a fictional story, including the trial's origin as a publicity stunt. In particular, the courtroom events and dialogue were lifted from trial transcripts with only minor edits for transitional purposes.

In researching the book I found myself presented with the most remarkable and colorful cast of characters a writer could ever hope for. Here is what happened to some of them after the trial ended.

.   .   .

Frances Robinson, unlike John Scopes, never did leave Dayton. Instead she followed his footsteps in another way, by becoming a teacher at Rhea Central High School. In 1940, at the age of twenty-four, she married Craig V. Gabbert, the school's football coach, and together the couple reared three children: Ann, Craig, and Leona. Frances lived for many years in the house where she grew up, across the street from the Rhea County Courthouse. She served as a docent at the courthouse and was popular as an interview subject during yearly reenactments of the Scopes trial. She died in 1996.

John Scopes received a master's degree in geology at the University of Chicago in 1927, after which he took a job as a geologist in Venezuela with the Gulf Oil Company. He spent most of his career at the United Gas Corporation. Scopes returned to Dayton only once, in 1960, and he never did like talking about the trial.

F. E. (Frank Earle) Robinson remained active in the civic life of Dayton until his death in 1957. He was one of the founders of Bryan College, an evangelical Christian college dedicated to the memory of William Jennings Bryan, and served as chairman of the board of trustees during the school's first thirty-five years, sometimes paying bills and teachers' salaries out of his own pocket.

H. L. Mencken had good reason to worry about his mother; she died just five months after the Scopes trial. In August 1930, following ten years of devoted friendship, he married Sara Haardt of Montgomery, Alabama. She died in 1935 of tubercular meningitis. Mencken was a journalist, critic, and linguistics expert, and his dispatches from Dayton are considered some of the finest of his career.

Clarence Darrow had hoped to appeal the Scopes case to the U.S. Supreme Court, but those plans came to an abrupt end in January 1927, when the Tennessee Supreme Court reversed John Scopes's conviction because the amount of the fine had been set by Judge Raulston rather than by the jury, as dictated by law. With the conviction overturned, there was nothing for Darrow to appeal, and the matter died quietly. Darrow turned his attention to other cases but maintained a close friendship with John Scopes for many years.

Edmund Duffy, who had been hired on H. L. Mencken's recommendation the year before the Scopes trial, went on to serve the *Baltimore Sun* as political cartoonist for nearly thirty years, winning numerous awards, including three Pulitzer Prizes.

Clarke Haggard Robinson, Frances's mother, continued to be a leader in the musical life of Dayton, encouraging many young people and opening her parlor to them for practice sessions. She died thirteen years after the Scopes trial, in 1938.

Wallace Clark ("Sonny") Robinson went to college at the University of the South in Sewanee, Tennessee, then served in the U.S. Army during World War II, rising to the rank of captain. He opened a branch store of Robinson's Drugs in the Rhea County town of Spring City, where he lived until his death in 1995.

John T. Raulston tried to parlay his fame as judge of the Scopes trial into higher political office but couldn't even manage reelection as judge in 1926. He died in 1956, at the age of ninety.

Sue Hicks was elected to the state legislature in 1935, defeating Walter White, and went on to a career as a judge.

George Rappleyea, who left Dayton a short time after the trial, was involved in several other publicity schemes, including the promotion of a plastic, molasses-based roofing and paving compound called Plas-Mo-Fault.

. . .

I had lots of help piecing together Frances's story.

Craig Gabbert provided insights, reference books, and, most important, his mother.

Dr. Richard Cornelius of Bryan College, along with his associate Tom Davis, supplied invaluable research help, as did Jerry Desmond and Norman Burns of the Chattanooga Regional History Museum. Dr. Carole Bucy checked for historical accuracy.

Eloise Purser Reed and Pauline Wilkey Greer shared their memories of the trial and of the Robinson family.

Vincent Fitzpatrick, curator of the H. L. Mencken Room at the Enoch Pratt Free Library in Baltimore, offered valuable insights into Mencken and showed me where to find the second-best crab cakes in Maryland.

My literary agents, Jodi Reamer and Amy Berkower of Writers House, believed in me from the beginning and put me in touch with Alyssa Eisner, my magnificent editor, who has unerring storytelling instincts and a heart for history.

My wife, Yvonne, put up with my early-morning alarm clock and my distracted glances during breakfast. My daughter, Maggie, who was three years old when I began writing the book, helped me type the manuscript, contributing words such as "SDKJFLSJDFKJ" and "GJSILDKA."

I will always be grateful to my parents, Paul and Ida Sue Kidd, who instilled in me a love of books and learning, and to three people who have shared with me their knowledge of writing: Marjorie Bruce, Steve Pritzker, and Mel Cebulash.

Here's a sneak peek
at Ronald Kidd's new book,
On Beale Street.
Coming Summer 2008

It was a good day at Poplar Tunes.

I was a regular there, a fifteen-year-old kid in blue jeans who showed up on summer afternoons and combed the record bins, looking for the latest hits by Hank Thompson and Kitty Wells. Mr. Novarese, the owner, would set aside records he thought I might like. He was behind the counter when I walked in that day.

"Hey, Johnny, I got one for you," he called. "It's the new Eddy Arnold."

Reaching into my pocket, I pulled out a few coins and a crumpled-up dollar bill, all the money I had in the world.

"Thanks, Mr. Novarese," I said, "but I'll be looking in the used bins today."

Poplar Tunes was the best record store in Memphis and was an easy bus ride from my house. There were rows of bins, with every kind of music from country to pop. My favorite part was the used section, where for a quarter you could pick up good records that had just a scratch or two.

As I started across the store, I noticed a familiar face. It was Ruth Ann Morris, who had been in my

English class the year before. I had spoken to her once or twice but wasn't sure she even knew my name. I knew hers. Ruth Ann had a smile that made my throat tighten, and she seemed to float a few inches off the ground. She was wearing a plain skirt and blouse, but to me she looked like royalty.

I was working up the nerve to say something, when my foot caught on one of the bins and I went sprawling in the aisle. I looked up and saw Ruth Ann gazing down at me. She smiled, but it wasn't mean. It was cool and beautiful, like always.

"You were in my English class," she said. "Aren't you Johnny Ross?"

I nodded. "You're Ruth Ann Morris."

Scrambling to my feet, I bumped my head on the bin. I lurched back a step. She stood on her tiptoes and reached for the bump on my head. My skin tingled where she touched it.

"Does it hurt?" she asked.

"Not now," I said. I blushed, and she smiled again.

"What happened?" said a voice behind me. It was Mr. Novarese.

"I bumped my head. It's okay."

"Let me see," he said.

Sighing, I tilted my head so he could look. He crouched down and examined the record bin.

"Seems fine," he said.

Ruth Ann stifled a giggle, then asked him, "Can you help me find a record? It's for my father's birthday."

"Johnny can help you," said Mr. Novarese. "He

may have a hard head, but he knows his music."

He went back to the counter, while I helped Ruth Ann check the bins. We looked at country records first, then moved to male vocalists. Her eyes lit up when she saw "Oh My Papa," a new single by Eddie Fisher.

"That's perfect!" she said.

Mr. Novarese rang up the record and put it in a bag. Ruth Ann started for the door, then hesitated.

"Thank you, Johnny," she said. She smiled. Then she was gone.

I spent more time looking through the bins, but my mind was still on Ruth Ann. I remembered her smile and the way she had touched me. Finally I picked out a couple of records and headed home.

"Hello, Memphis! Bob Neal here, frying eggs on the sidewalk and bringing you the top country hits. That was a new one from Webb Pierce."

I sat on our front steps, drinking an Orange Crush and listening to music. Sometimes on hot days I would bring the radio out onto our porch, trying to get away from the heat inside. A few people in the neighborhood had air-conditioning, but we didn't. Arthur Chapman did. He was my mother's boss. He owned half of downtown Memphis. Mr. Chapman had one of the biggest houses in town, and my mother and I lived in a cottage at the back of his property.

Bob Neal talked about Goody's Headache Powder, then played more music. As I listened, a young man came around the corner of our house. He was a few years older than me, with skin the color of caramel. He glanced around, as if sizing the place up.

"What are you doing?" I asked.

I half expected him to run. Instead, he looked up at me. "You live here?"

"I said, what are you doing?"

"I'm supposed to trim your bushes," he said. "But if you live here, seems like you should do it."

"Where's Will?" I asked. Will was a combination gardener, handyman, and driver for Arthur Chapman.

The young man said, "Will's in the garage, working on the cars."

"Maybe I'll go get him."

"You do that," he said.

I stared at him, and he stared back.

He said, "Who are you?"

"Johnny Ross."

He nodded, then disappeared around the corner and came back holding a pair of gardening shears. He held them out to me. "You'll need these."

I didn't move. He shrugged. "Can't say I didn't try."

He turned to the bush. Holding the shears with a left-handed grip, he clipped off a few small branches.

"You're new," I said.

"Score one for the white boy."

"You talk different. Not just your accent."

He shook his head. "People in Memphis, they don't know what real Negroes sound like. We have opinions. We know what we want. We don't smile and shuffle."

He lowered the shears and held out his hand. "I'm Lamont Turner. From Chicago."

I shook his hand. I didn't know what else to do. Then I thought of something. "Turner? Are you any relation to Will?"

"Score two for the white boy. He's my father."

"I didn't know Will had a son."

"Now you do," he said.

"How did you get here?" I asked.

"Drove."

"You know what I mean."

He said, "Will Turner used to be married to my mother. They split after I was born, and we moved to Chicago. That's where I was raised. Early this year my mother was out of work. She has relatives in Memphis, and they got her a job, if you can call it that. A few weeks ago we moved back here."

"What's the job?" I asked.

"She's a maid. I bet you're impressed. Mother's a maid, father's a grunt."

"What about you?"

"I just finished high school," he said. "My father got me this job. Assistant grunt. This is my first day."

"You don't sound too happy about it."

"I'm happy about the money."

Money. It was something I thought about a lot. I guess that's the way it is when you don't have much of it. I thought about it now—how it would feel in my hand, what I would buy with it.

"Maybe I should get a job," I said.

"You *want* a job? Man, what's wrong with you?

You got the American dream—no school, no work, just summer stretching out all day long."

"And night," I said. "I like it at night."

He smiled, looking someplace I couldn't see. "You like the nighttime, try the South Side of Chicago. People on the streets. Laughing, drinking. Listening to music. I used to drive down there every chance I got."

I said, "You have a car?"

"Thirty-eight Ford. I'll take you for a ride sometime."

I hesitated. He saw it in my face.

"What's wrong, you scared? White boy don't want to be seen with a Nee-gro?"

Someone called, "Hey, Johnny!"

I looked around and saw Trey Chapman, Mr. Chapman's son. He was eighteen, with blond hair, big shoulders, and a bigger grin. Trey had just graduated from a fancy boarding school. Now that he was back home, he liked to drive through town in his Cadillac convertible. Sometimes he would hang around the house, trying to stir things up.

When Trey got closer, he shot me a smile that wasn't a smile. "What are you doing? Hanging out with the help?"

"I guess so," I said.

Trey turned to Lamont. "What are you staring at?"

"You," said Lamont.

Trey stepped toward him, so their noses were almost touching. Lamont didn't budge.

"This ain't Chicago," said Trey. "It's Memphis."

"So?" said Lamont.

Trey said, "You don't understand how it works around here."

"Maybe you could explain."

"This is how it works," said Trey.

He gave Lamont a hard shove. Lamont staggered back and fell to the ground. Dropping the gardening shears, he jumped to his feet, face flushed. He took a step toward Trey.

Trey grinned. "One more step and you're fired. Your father's fired. Your mother, too. Do it, man. Come on, take a step."

Lamont leaned forward, his hands working.

Trey said, "Or you could go for the jackpot. Hit me. Imagine how that would feel. Just one swing. You can do it, I know you can."

Lamont clenched his fists. Sweat dripped from his chin.

"Touch me," said Trey, "and your life's over."

Lamont reached for him. Trey's grin slipped, just for a moment. Then Lamont stopped, and Trey's grin came back.

Lamont said, "Another time, another place. I'll get you."

"You watch it, boy," said Trey.

Lamont gazed at him. Then, straightening his shoulders, he picked up the gardening shears and headed off.

Trey called after him. "Hey!"

Lamont turned around.

"Welcome to Memphis," said Trey.

He watched Lamont leave, then took a pack of cigarettes from his pocket, shook one out, and lit it. Squinting throught the smoke, he reached down and adjusted the dial on my radio. There was static, then the voice of Patti Page, singing a pop tune.

"You like that music?" I asked.

"Naw," he said. "But leave it on that station. WHBQ, at 560. Tonight at ten o'clock, Dewey Phillips comes on. He's got a show called *Red Hot and Blue*."

"You mean, like the flag?"

"No, man. *Red* Hot *and Blue*. Blue as in the blues. B.B. King. Big Mama Thornton. Rufus Thomas. Don't tell me you've never heard of them."

I shrugged.

Trey lowered his voice and looked around. "They're Negroes. They have their own kind of music. It's incredible."

"I thought you didn't like Negroes," I said.

"I love Negroes. Can't you tell? Anyway, I'm not planning to invite one home. I just like their music."

I said, "Is Dewey Phillips a Negro?"

Trey laughed. "A Negro? He's as white as you or me. But not normal white. He's loud white. Jumping white. Crazy white."

Trey took a long pull from his cigarette, then crushed it out on the porch next to me.

"Just listen tonight," he said. "You'll see."

He shot me a grin, then moved off across the yard.

That night my mother made cornbread and black-eyed peas. She was tall, with wavy brown hair, dark eyes, and a forehead with a permanent set of wrinkles.

She had put an apron on over her business suit. As she moved around the kitchen, I could tell that her mind was still downtown, at work. She brought our food to the kitchen table and asked distractedly, "How was your day?"

I didn't say anything about Ruth Ann or Trey. I did tell her about Poplar Tunes, and I mentioned Will's son.

She looked up at me, her attention suddenly riveted. "Will's son?"

"Lamont. He's from Chicago."

I told her what he was like and how he had come to Memphis. I was surprised to realize that she already seemed to know about him.

She shook her head, worried. "Stay away from that boy."

"From Lamont? Why?"

"Just do as I say."

I dug in to the cornbread. She took a sip of coffee, eyeing me thoughtfully.

"I heard you come in last night," she said. "You were out late again, weren't you?"

"Aw, Mom."

For as long as I could remember, my mother had fallen asleep early, tired from work. I'd gotten into the habit of going out while she slept. Most of the time she didn't even know it.

"I don't like you running around at night," she said. "It's dangerous."

"I'm not little anymore. I'm fifteen."

"What do you do out there?" she asked.

"Nothing."

"You're going to get in trouble. I don't want to be waked up some night by the police."

"Thanks for the vote of confidence," I said.

"I mean it, Johnny. Find something else to do. Take up a hobby."

I remembered my conversation with Lamont. "Maybe I should get a job."

"A job?"

"We could use the money."

"That's crazy. You're a boy. It's summer. You're supposed to be having fun. Besides, I've got a perfectly good job."

"He hardly pays you anything," I said. "How long have you been with him? Twenty years? You practically run the place."

"Mr. Chapman's been good to us. He lets us stay in this house."

"And isn't it great," I said.

"What's that supposed to mean?"

"Come on, Mom. What are we doing here? This is the richest neighborhood in town. We don't have money. We don't have a big house. We don't belong. It's a pretend life. The kids at school know it. They laugh at me."

"Don't pay any attention to them."

"Wake up, Mom. You're dreaming. I'm not Trey Chapman. I never will be. At least let me make some money. Even Lamont has money."

She set her jaw and went back to eating. Shaking

my head, I got up from the table and took my dishes to the sink, then went into my room and closed the door.

When I came out later she had fallen asleep on the sofa. I covered her with a quilt and went back to my room. Sitting on the bed, I turned on the radio and adjusted the dial to 560. A voice came flying out.

Deegaw! Dewey Phillips comin' at you, just flat fixin' to bring you the hottest thing in the country, Red Hot and Blue, *on WHBQ in Memphis, Tennessee. Wake up out there, just get ready. We're gonna play the first record for Denice, for Percy, for J.V., for Bernice, for Beulah, for Effie, for Oliver. We're gonna flat "Dig That Boogie" by Piano Red. Aw, just set on it, Red. If you can't set on it, lay on it.*

Somebody started pounding on a piano and singing. *"Let's dig that boogie, let's dig that boogie."*

Dewey Phillips talked over the music, laughing, singing along. The music ended, and he kept on going.

The next portion of Red Hot and Blue *comes to you courtesy of Lansky Brothers Clothing, down on Beale Street. They got easy credit. Just pay for it while you're wearin' it out. Go on and get you a wheelbarrow full of horseshoes and run 'em right through the front door. Just kick it down and tell 'em Dewey Phillips sent you. Yes sir, Lansky's. Down on Beale Street, where there's music every night. We got Piano Red at the Club House, Little Laura Dukes at the Midway, Rosco Gordon at Peewee's Saloon. Hey, Rosco, you there? Come on in, baby. No more doggin'. You tell 'em.*

As he talked, a laid-back shuffling tune started, with a saxophone and a singer whose voice was soft and hoarse. *"No more doggin', foolin' around with you."*

The music played. Dewey Phillips talked. There was more music and more talking. Through it all I sat on my bed, not moving.

There was something about that voice, that music. I'd never heard anything like it. Half the time I couldn't understand the words, but it didn't matter. It was pure feeling. It was life, spilling out of the speaker and into my house. There were people, like the ones who worked in mansions up and down the street, like Will, like Lamont.

It was a place. It was a world—in the air, in my mind. And it had a name. Beale Street. Beale Street, where there's music every night.

I had always heard about Beale Street. I'd been there a few times on my way to someplace else. It was downtown for Negroes. They had their own stores, restaurants, theaters. It was right next to the white downtown, but it could have been miles away. We had our world and they had theirs, close by, related, parallel but never touching. There was black. There was white. But there was never gray. That's just the way it was in Memphis.

I thought about Beale Street, about the music and the people. I wondered what it was like after dark.

READ THE BRAIN-KICKING
NEW YORK TIMES **BESTSELLERS:**

AND DON'T MISS THE FOURTH BOOK:

PUBLISHED BY SIMON PULSE

GARY PAULSEN
Three-time Newbery Honor author

Newbery Honor Book

Newbery Honor Book

From Simon Pulse • Published by Simon & Schuster

RONALD KIDD is the author of *Dunker*, winner of a Children's Choice Award; *Second Fiddle*, an Edgar Award nominee and a Library of Congress Children's Book of the Year; *Who Is Felix the Great?*, a Books for the Teen Age listing; and *Sizzle & Splat*, a *School Library Journal* Best Book of the Year. He is a two-time O'Neill playwright. He lives with his wife and daughter in Nashville, Tennessee. Ron is currently at work on his next teen novel, about race relations and rock 'n' roll music in 1950s Memphis.

Made in the USA
San Bernardino, CA
26 April 2016